DISCARDED
Goshen Public Library

FAR OUT
FAIRY TALES

STONE ARCH BOOKS
a capstone imprint

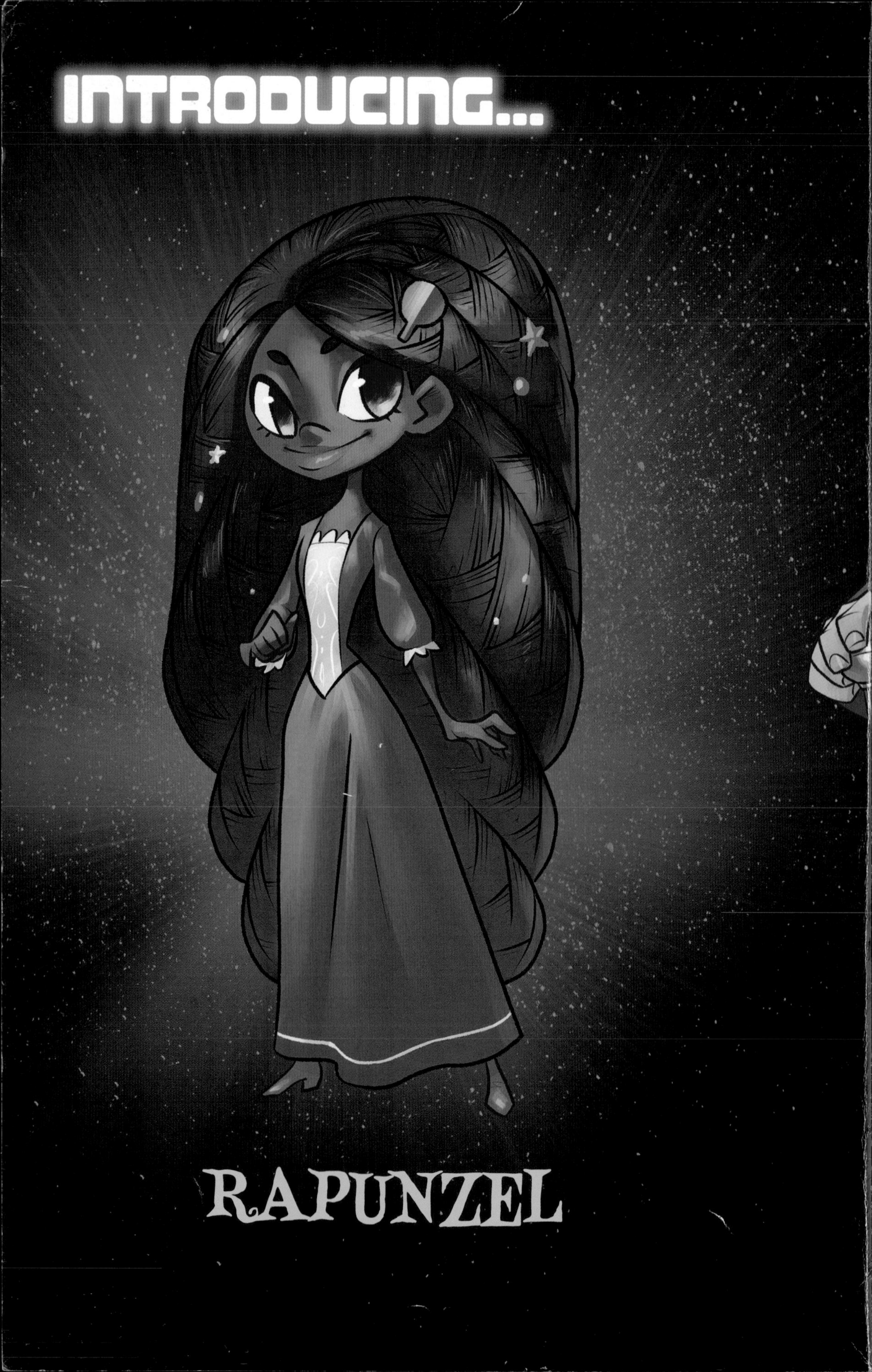
INTRODUCING...
RAPUNZEL

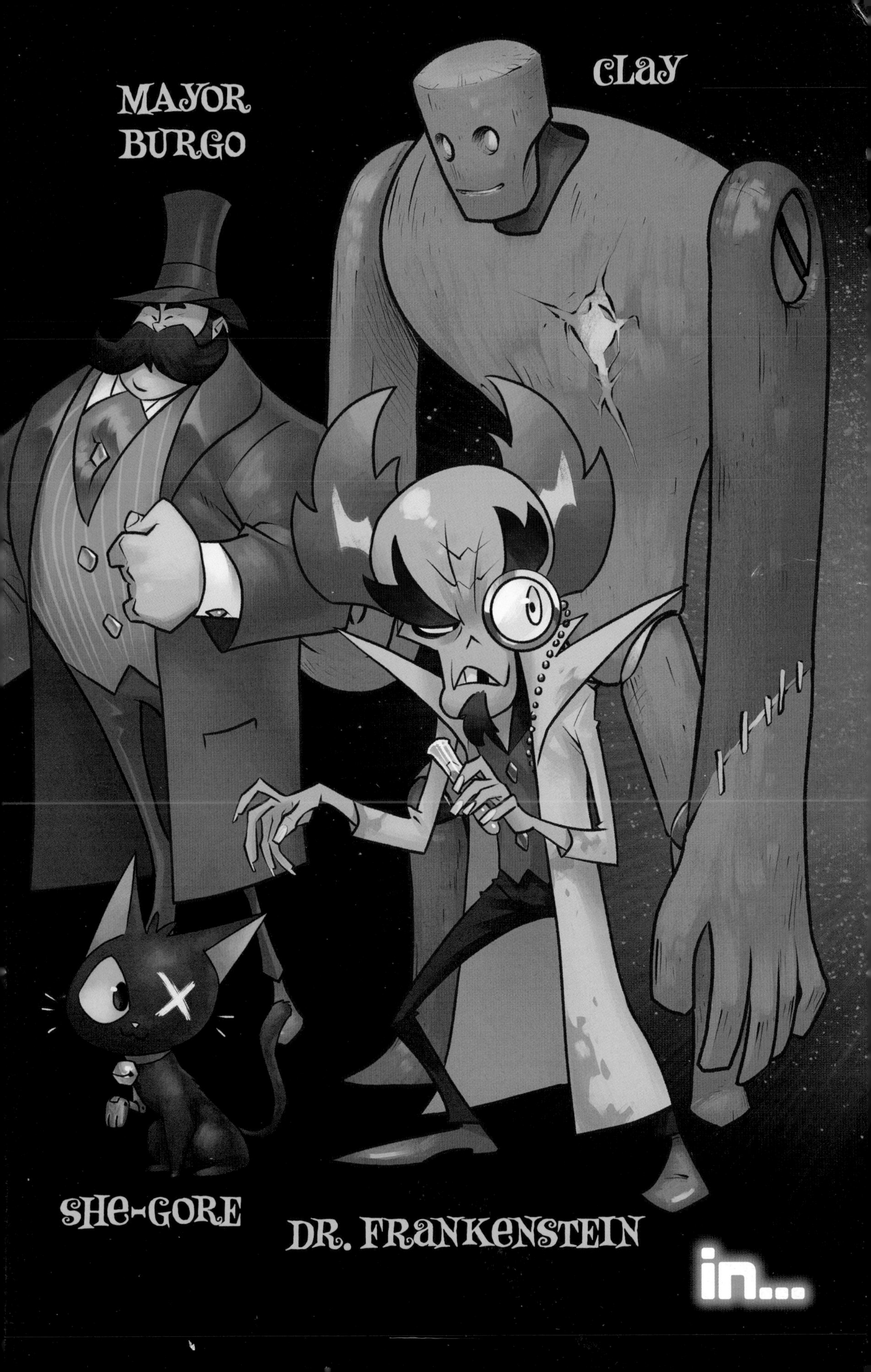
MAJOR BURGO
CLAY
SHE-GORE
DR. FRANKENSTEIN
in...

Far Out Fairy Tales is published by
Stone Arch Books
a Capstone imprint
1710 Roe Crest Drive
North Mankato, Minnesota 56003
www.capstonepub.com

Cataloging-in-Publication Data is
available at the Library of Congress
website.
ISBN: 978-1-4965-8395-6 (hardcover)
ISBN: 978-1-4965-8444-1 (paperback)
ISBN: 978-1-4965-8400-7 (eBook PDF)

Summary: After a chemical spill in
Dr. Frankenstein's lab, Rapunzel's hair
has grown to extreme lengths . . . and
it's alive! But her long locks weren't
the only thing animated that stormy
night. A lightning strike also shocked
life into a clay figure. Now Frankenstein
is locking his two creations away. Can
Rapunzel and her friend ever escape the
mad scientist's tower?

Designed by Hilary Wacholz
Edited by Abby Huff
Lettered by Jaymes Reed

*For Sara and the gentle ghost
of her father, Boris Karloff—M.P.*

Printed and bound in the USA.
PA70

FAR OUT FAIRY TALES

RAPUNZEL VS. FRANKENSTEIN

A GRAPHIC NOVEL

BY MARTIN POWELL

ILLUSTRATED BY OMAR LOZANO

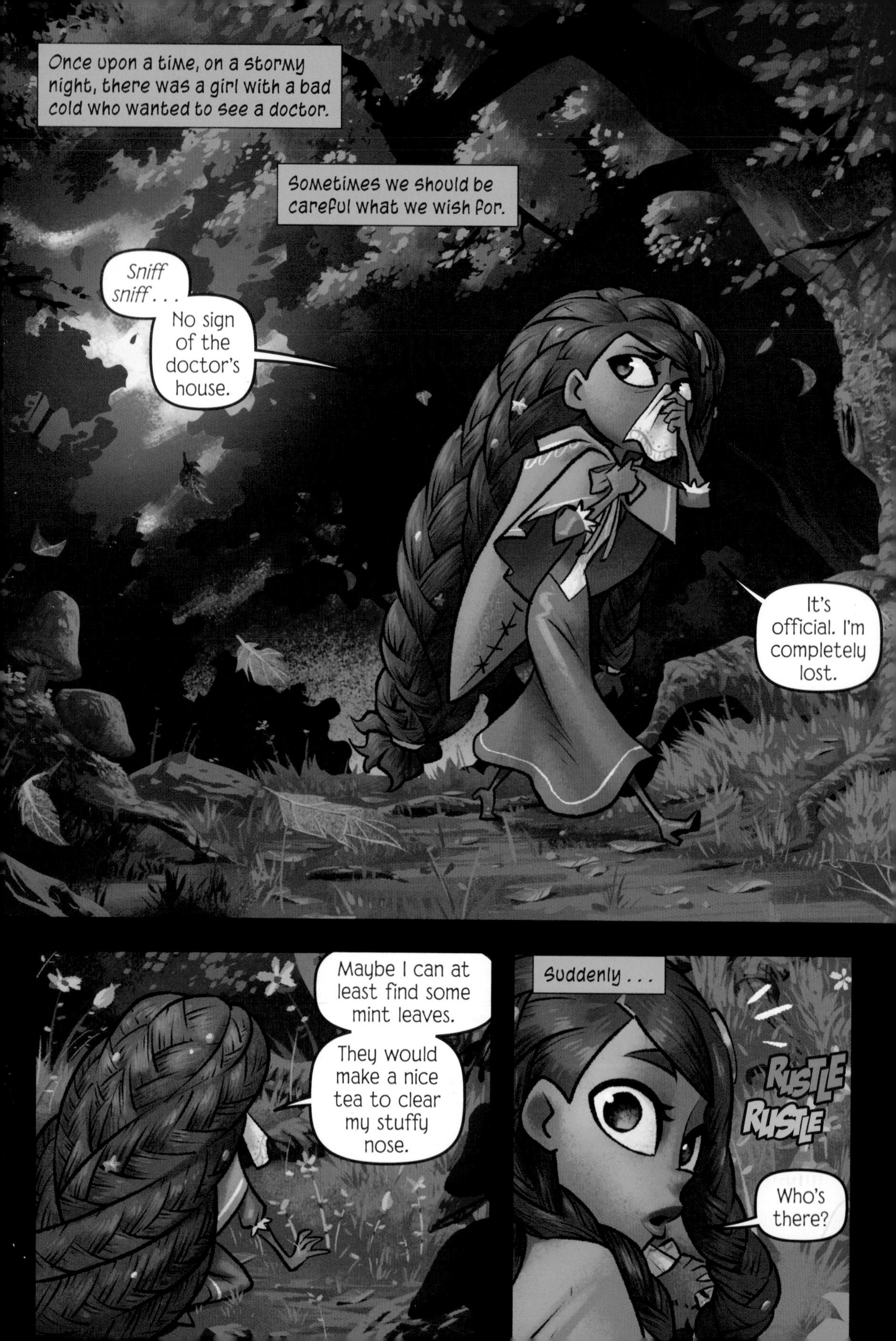
Once upon a time, on a stormy night, there was a girl with a bad cold who wanted to see a doctor.
Sometimes we should be careful what we wish for.
Sniff sniff . . .
No sign of the doctor's house.
It's official. I'm completely lost.
Maybe I can at least find some mint leaves.
They would make a nice tea to clear my stuffy nose.
Suddenly . . .
RUSTLE RUSTLE
Who's there?

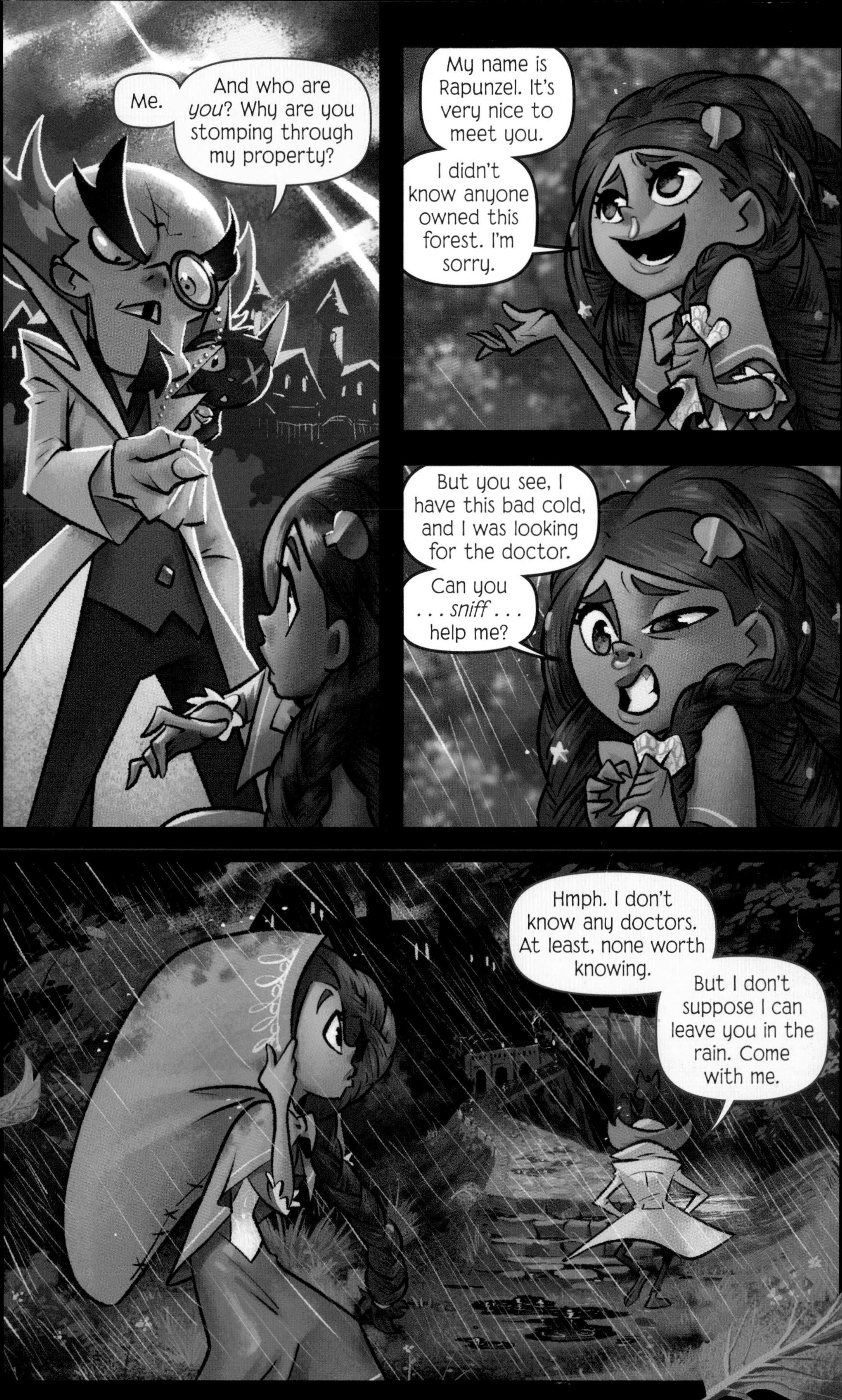

And who are *you*? Why are you stomping through my property?
Me.
My name is Rapunzel. It's very nice to meet you.
I didn't know anyone owned this forest. I'm sorry.
But you see, I have this bad cold, and I was looking for the doctor.
Can you . . . *sniff* . . . help me?
Hmph. I don't know any doctors. At least, none worth knowing.
But I don't suppose I can leave you in the rain. Come with me.

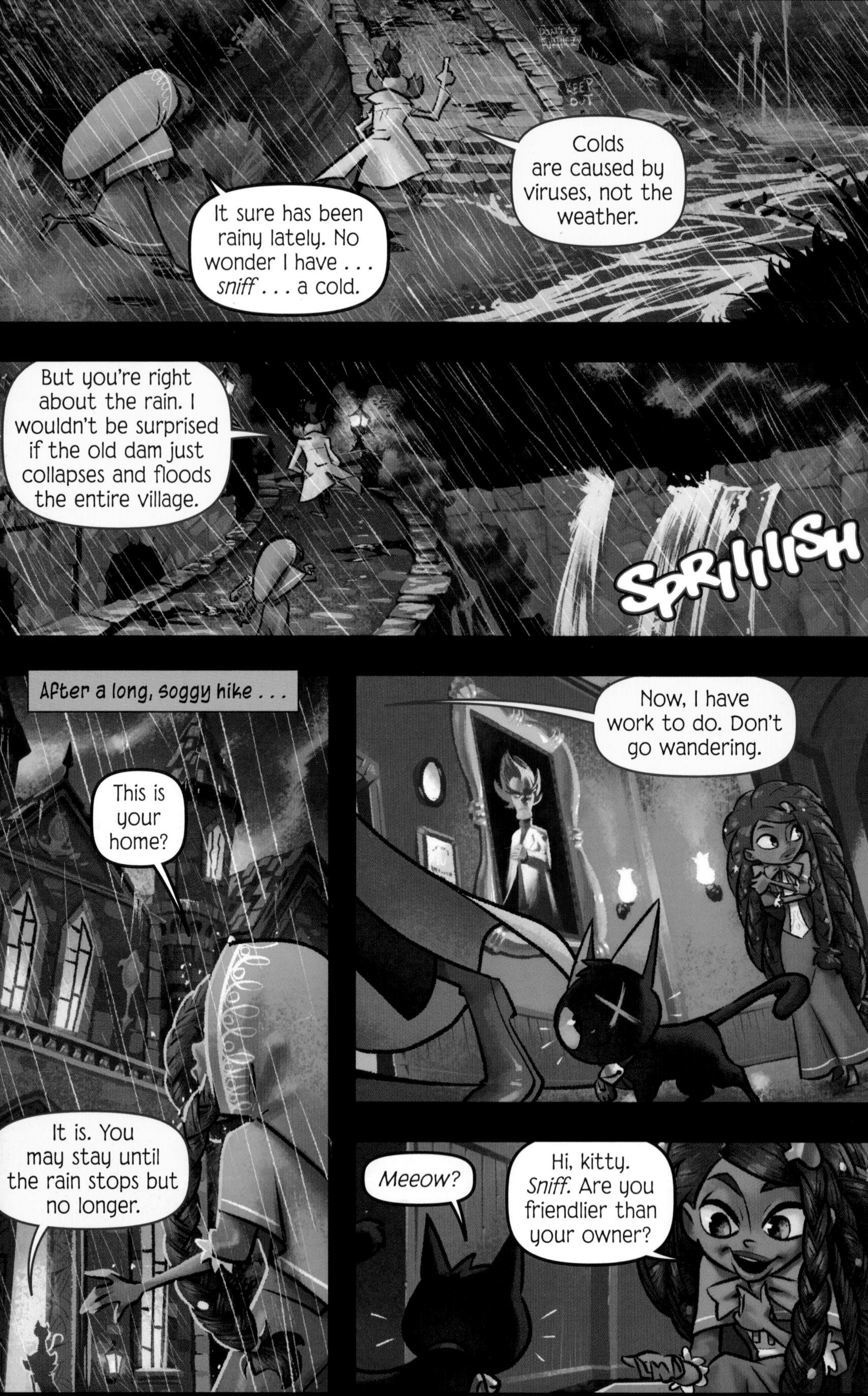
It sure has been rainy lately. No wonder I have . . . *sniff* . . . a cold.
Colds are caused by viruses, not the weather.
But you're right about the rain. I wouldn't be surprised if the old dam just collapses and floods the entire village.
SPRIIIIISH
After a long, soggy hike . . .
This is your home?
It is. You may stay until the rain stops but no longer.
Now, I have work to do. Don't go wandering.
Hi, kitty. *Sniff.* Are you friendlier than your owner?
Meeow?

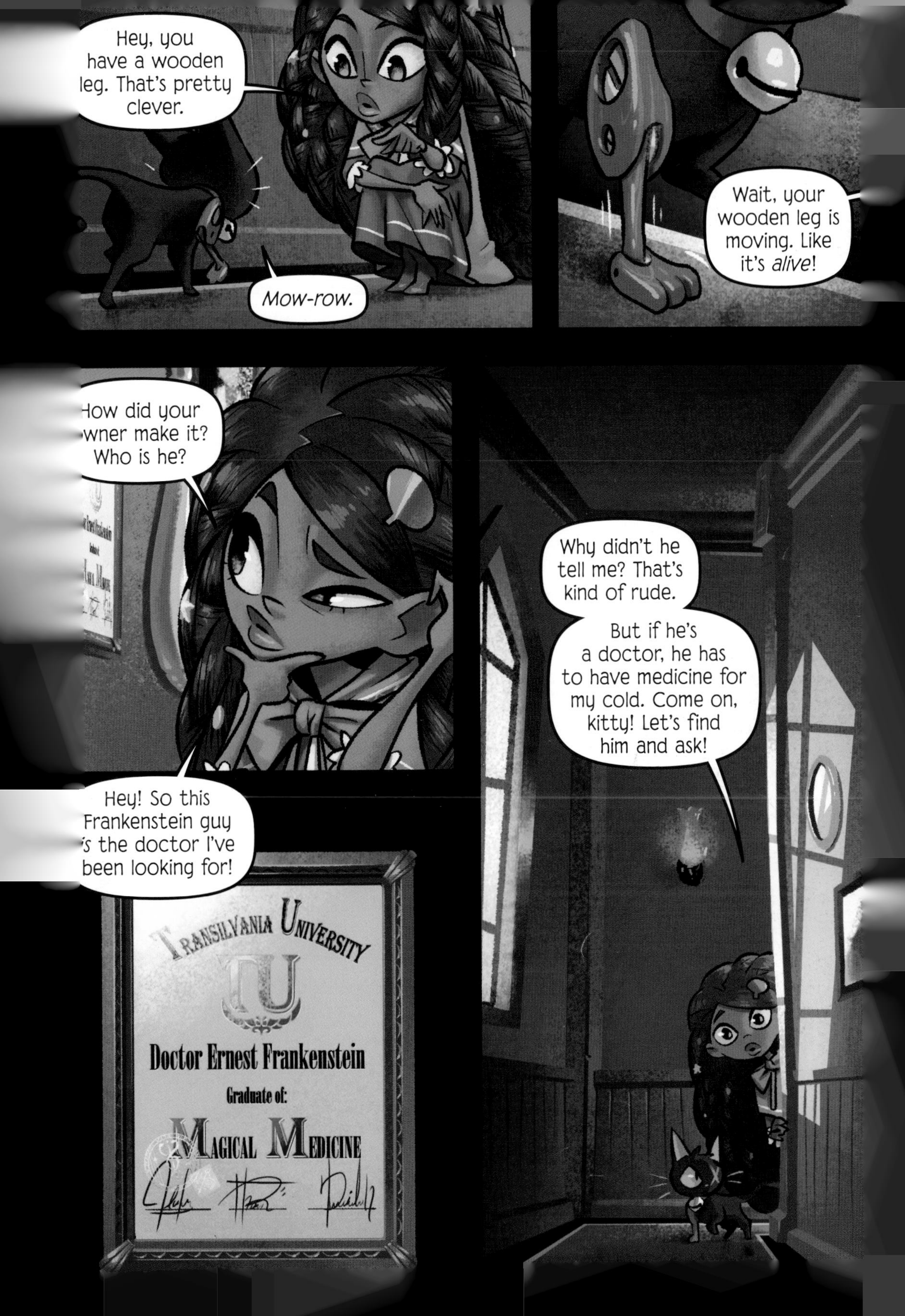
Hey, you have a wooden leg. That's pretty clever.
Mow-row.
Wait, your wooden leg is moving. Like it's *alive*!
How did your wner make it? Who is he?
Hey! So this Frankenstein guy 's the doctor I've been looking for!
TRANSILVANIA UNIVERSITY
TU
Doctor Ernest Frankenstein
Graduate of:
MAGICAL MEDICINE
Why didn't he tell me? That's kind of rude.
But if he's a doctor, he has to have medicine for my cold. Come on, kitty! Let's find him and ask!

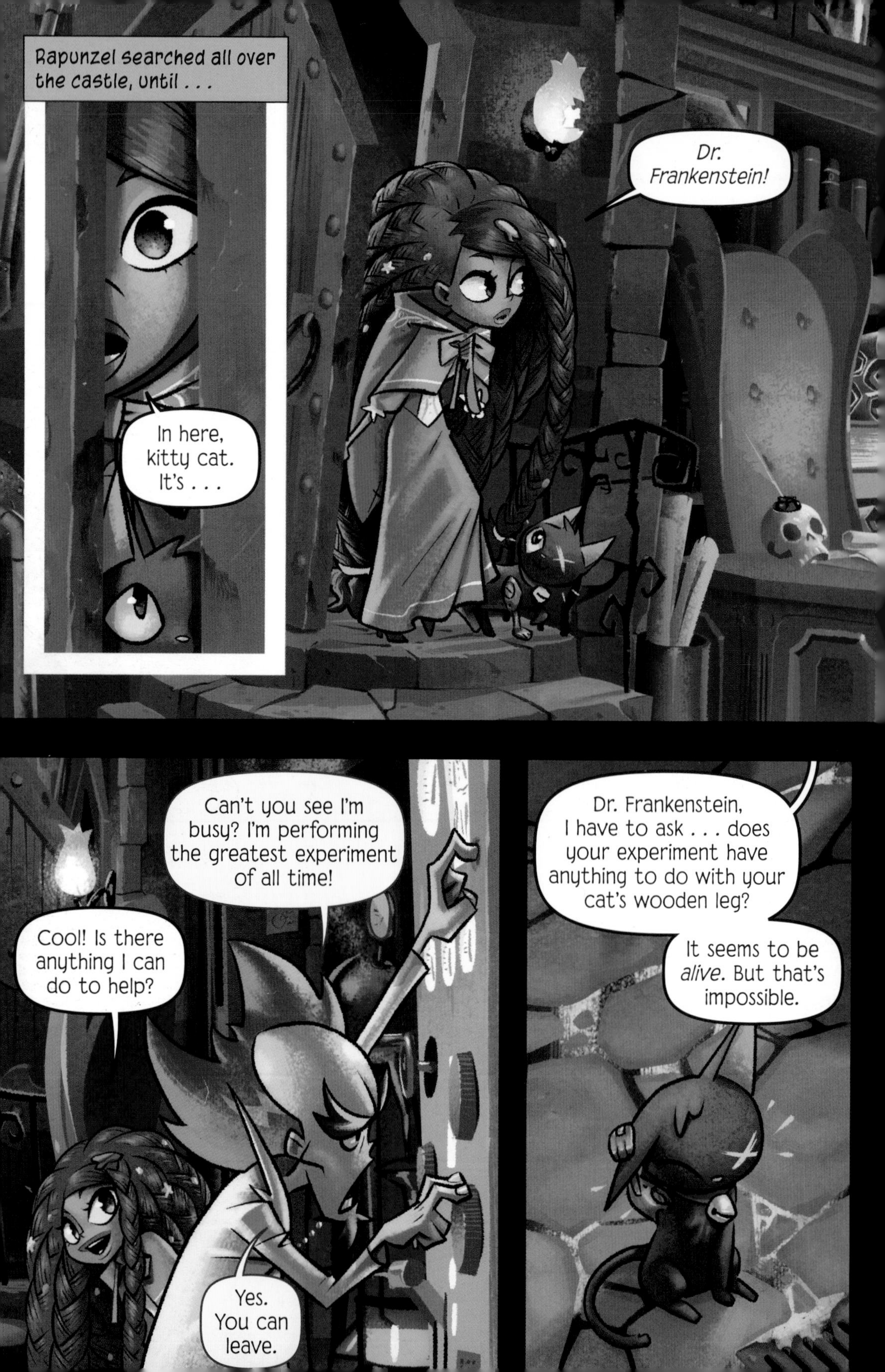

Rapunzel searched all over the castle, until . . .
In here, kitty cat. It's . . .
Dr. Frankenstein!
Can't you see I'm busy? I'm performing the greatest experiment of all time!
Cool! Is there anything I can do to help?
Yes. You can leave.
Dr. Frankenstein, I have to ask . . . does your experiment have anything to do with your cat's wooden leg?
It seems to be *alive*. But that's impossible.

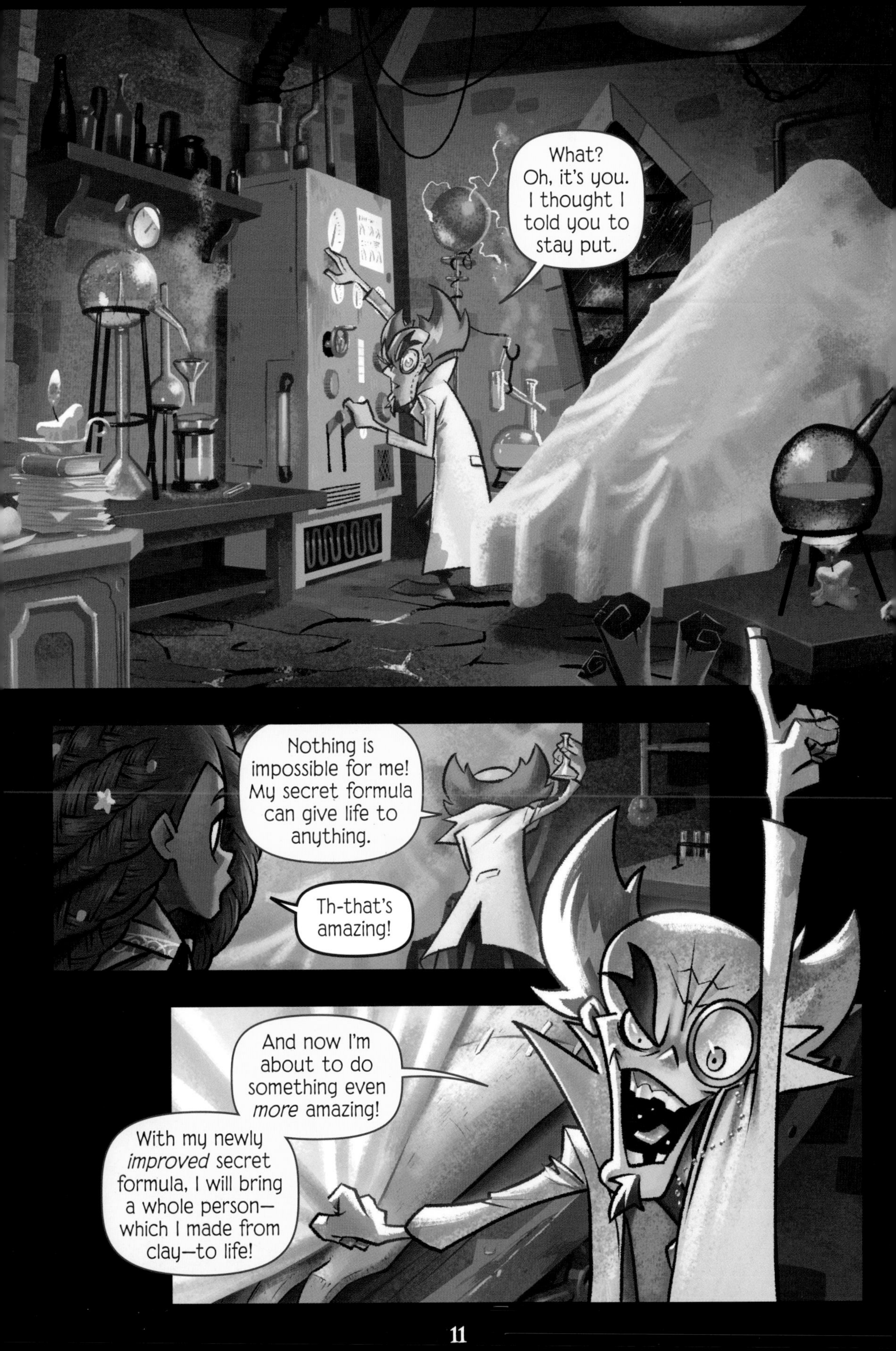

What? Oh, it's you. I thought I told you to stay put.
Nothing is impossible for me! My secret formula can give life to anything.
Th-that's amazing!
And now I'm about to do something even *more* amazing!
With my newly *improved* secret formula, I will bring a whole person—which I made from clay—to life!

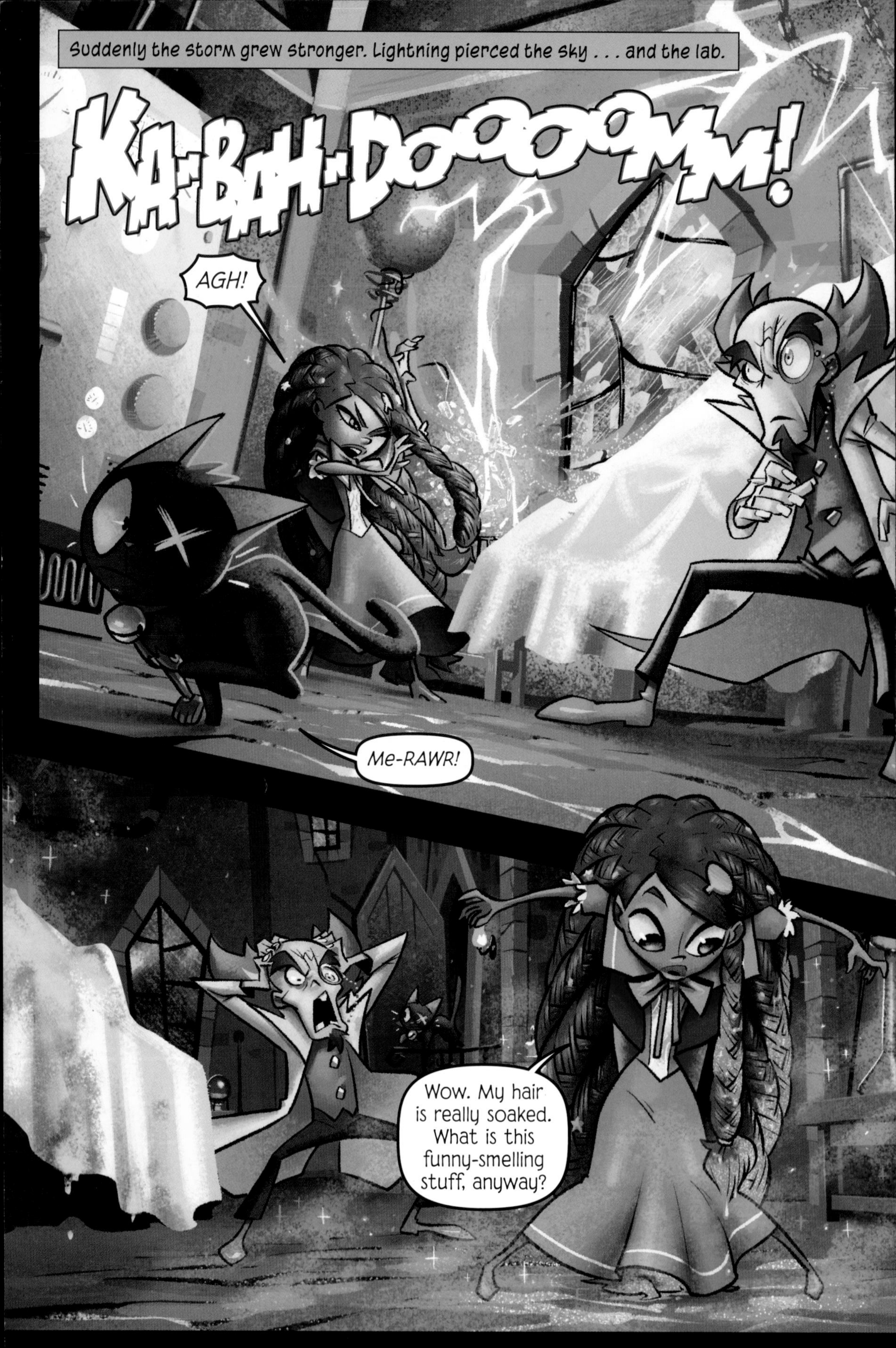
Suddenly the storm grew stronger. Lightning pierced the sky . . . and the lab.
KA-BAH-DOOOOOMM!
AGH!
Me-RAWR!
Wow. My hair is really soaked. What is this funny-smelling stuff, anyway?

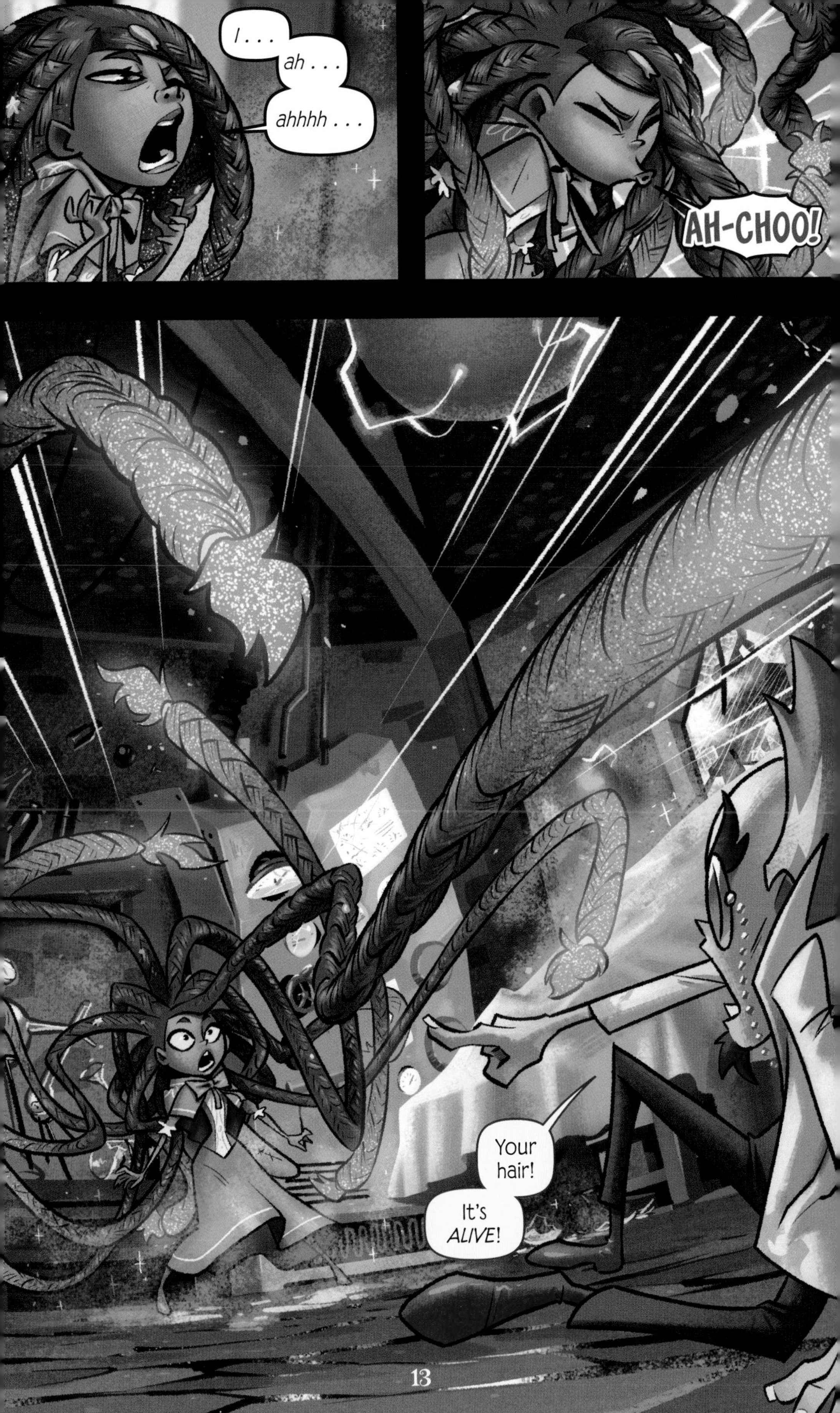
I . . .
ah . . .
ahhhh . . .
AH-CHOO!
Your hair!
It's *ALIVE*!

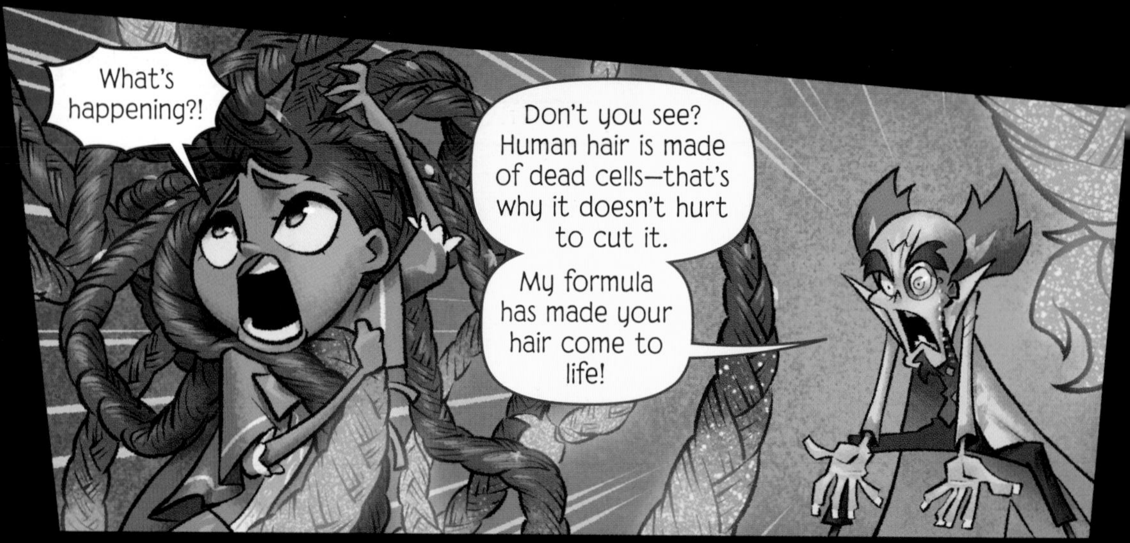
What's happening?!
Don't you see? Human hair is made of dead cells—that's why it doesn't hurt to cut it.
My formula has made your hair come to life!

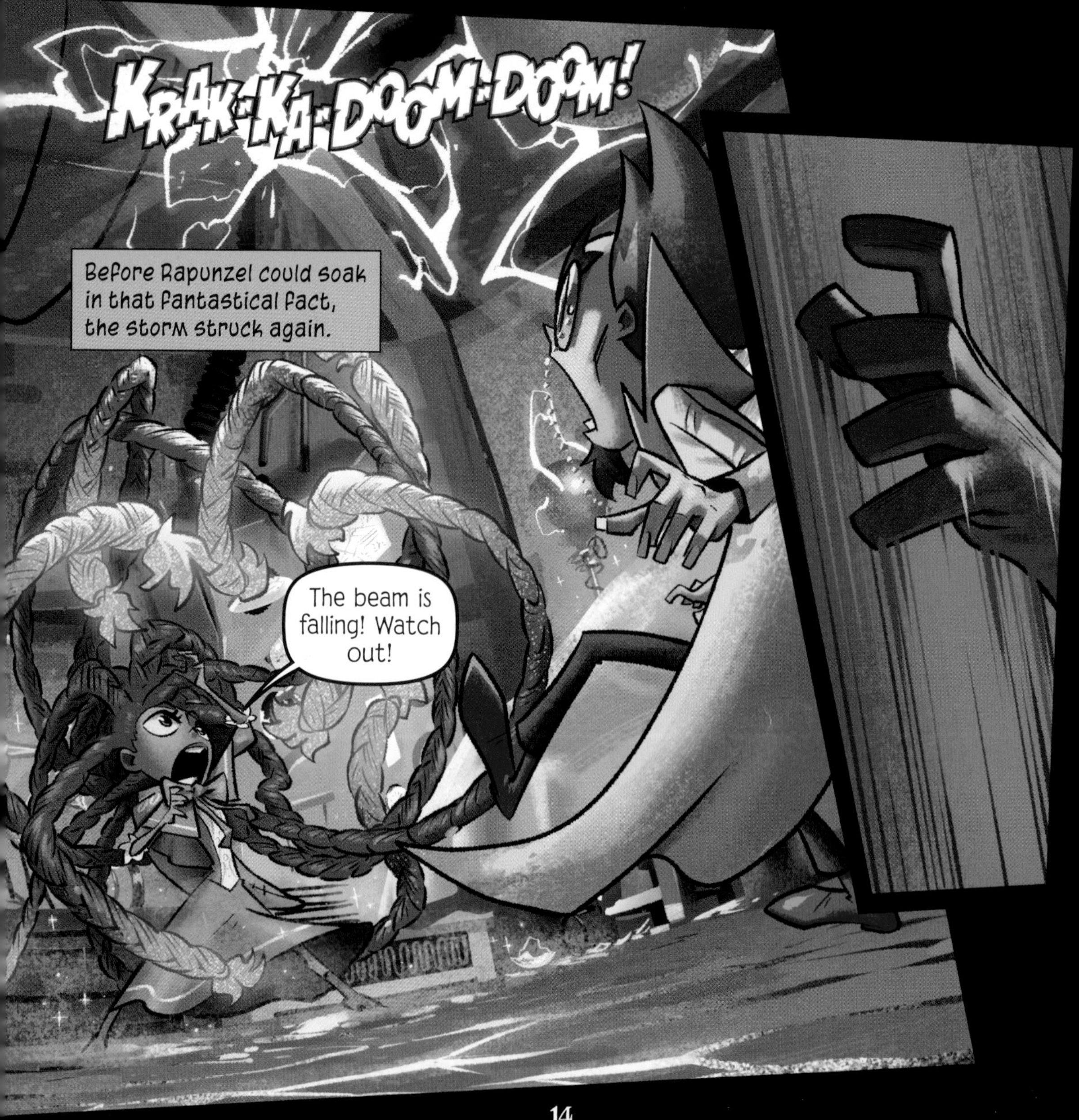
KRAK-KA-DOOM-DOOM!
Before Rapunzel could soak in that fantastical fact, the storm struck again.
The beam is falling! Watch out!

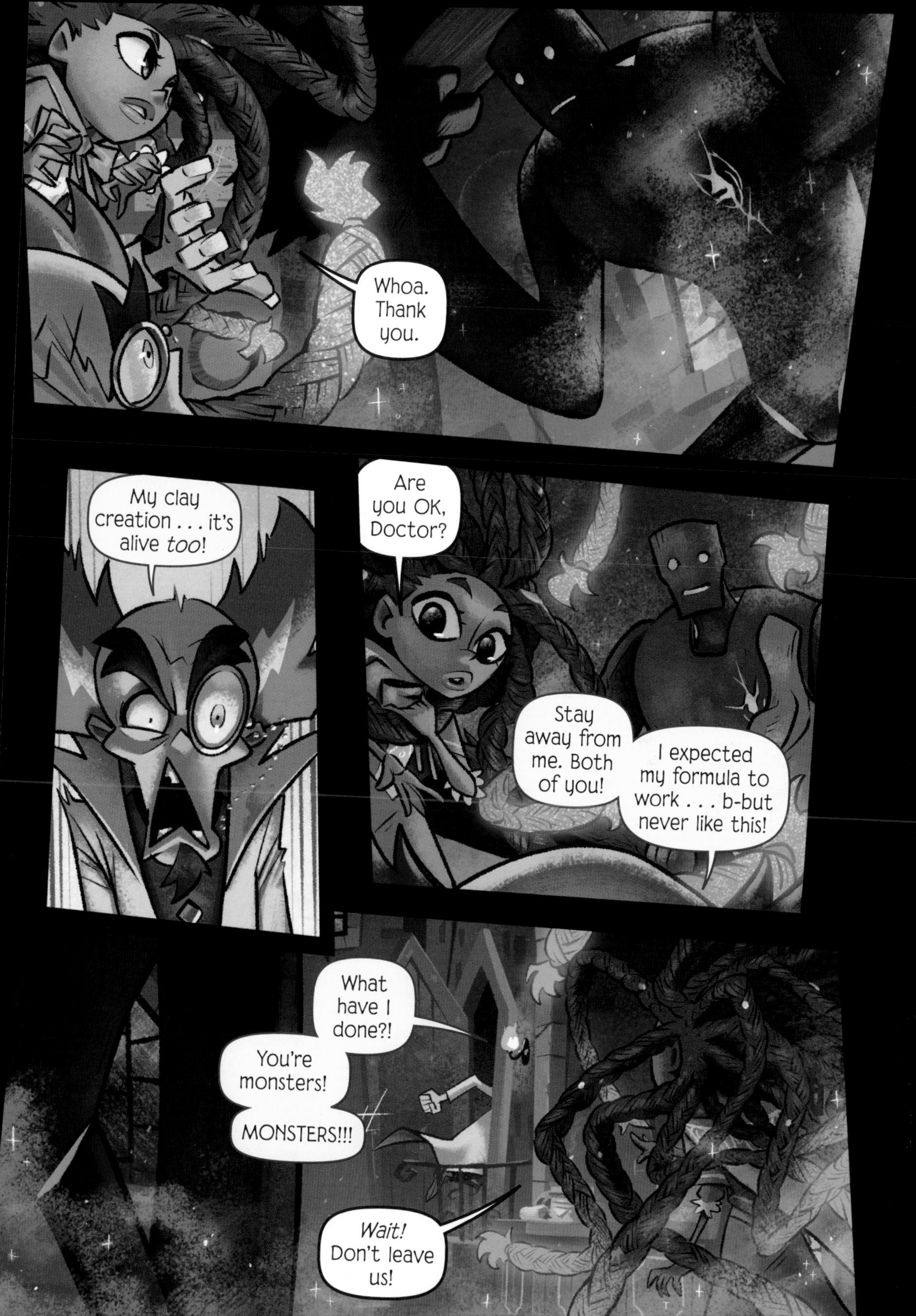
Whoa. Thank you.
My clay creation . . . it's alive *too*!
Are you OK, Doctor?
Stay away from me. Both of you!
I expected my formula to work . . . b-but never like this!
What have I done?!
You're monsters!
MONSTERS!!!
Wait! Don't leave us!

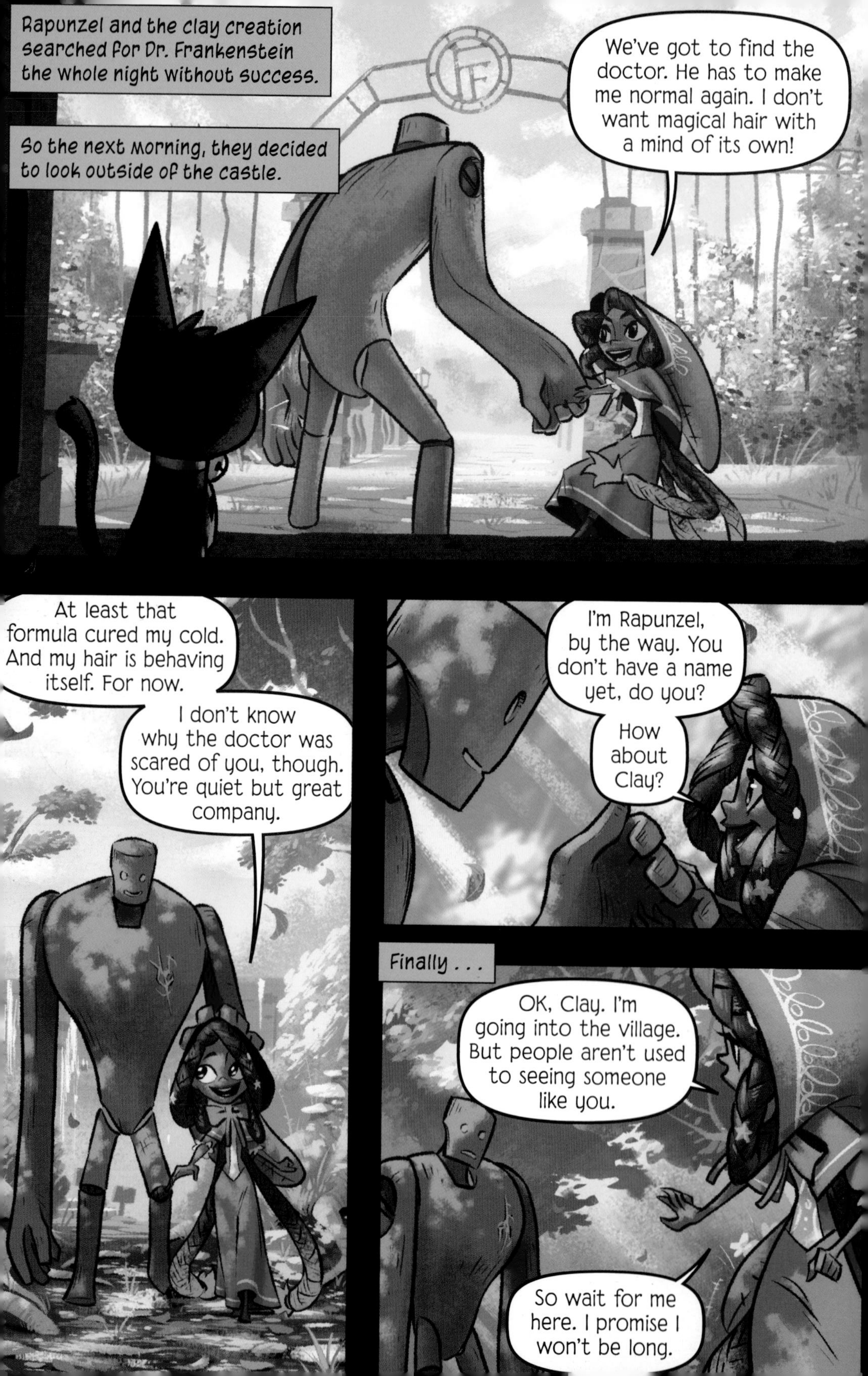

Rapunzel and the clay creation searched for Dr. Frankenstein the whole night without success.
So the next morning, they decided to look outside of the castle.
We've got to find the doctor. He has to make me normal again. I don't want magical hair with a mind of its own!
At least that formula cured my cold. And my hair is behaving itself. For now.
I don't know why the doctor was scared of you, though. You're quiet but great company.
I'm Rapunzel, by the way. You don't have a name yet, do you?
How about Clay?
Finally . . .
OK, Clay. I'm going into the village. But people aren't used to seeing someone like you.
So wait for me here. I promise I won't be long.

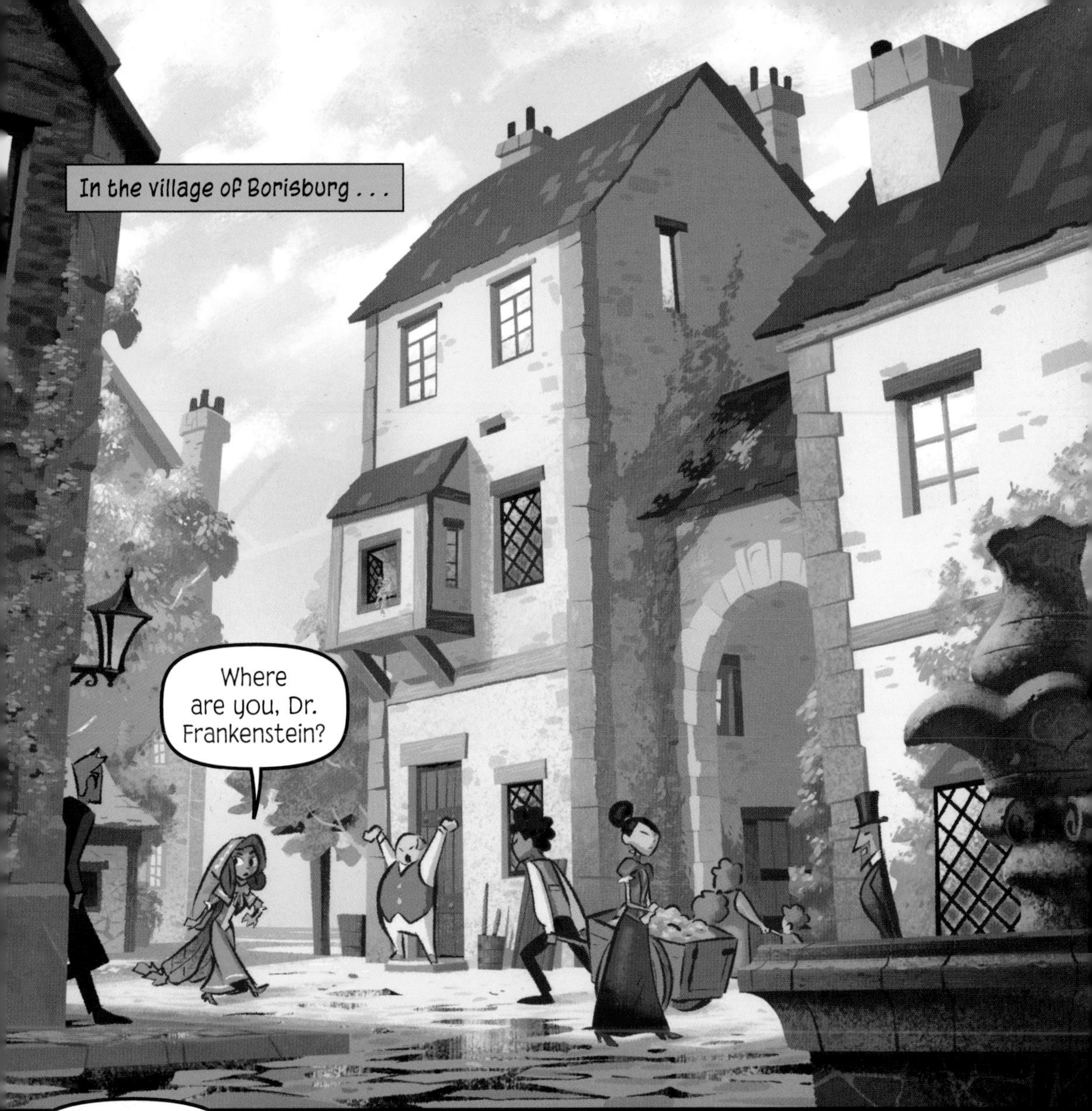
In the village of Borisburg . . .
Where are you, Dr. Frankenstein?

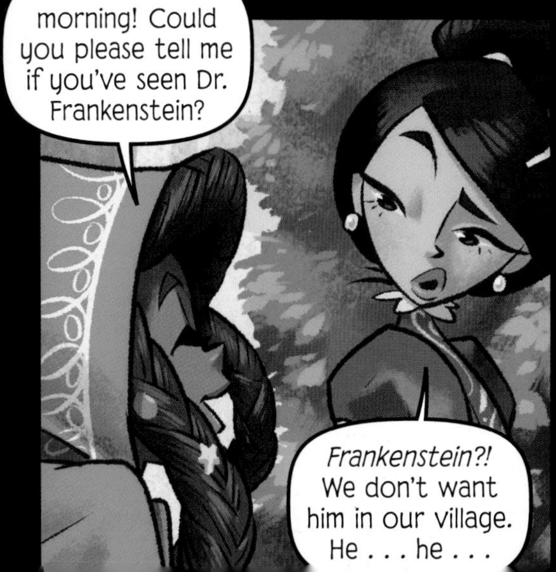
Good morning! Could you please tell me if you've seen Dr. Frankenstein?
Frankenstein?! We don't want him in our village. He . . . he . . .

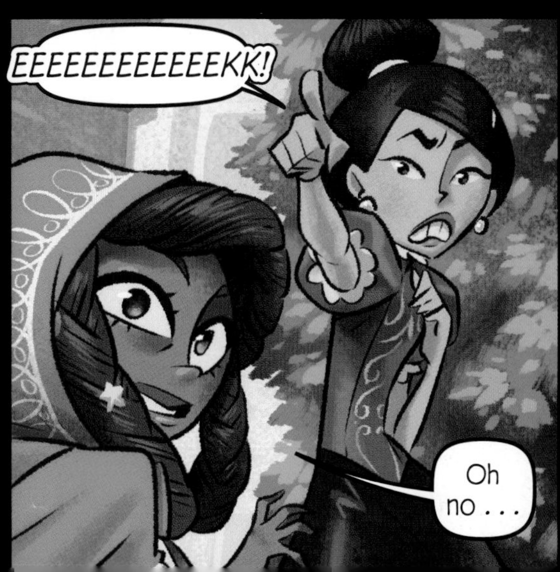
EEEEEEEEEEEEKK!
Oh no . . .

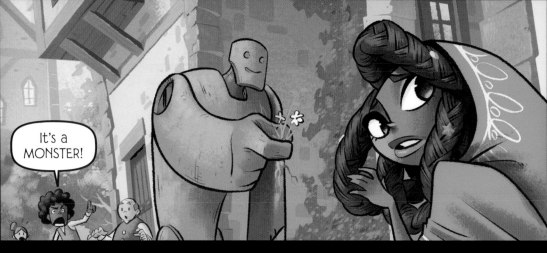

It's a MONSTER!

No, you're wrong! He's not a monster. He's as gentle as a kitten!

It's another of Frankenstein's monsters!

We don't want you here!

Yeah!

FREAK!

Please, stop. You're scaring him!

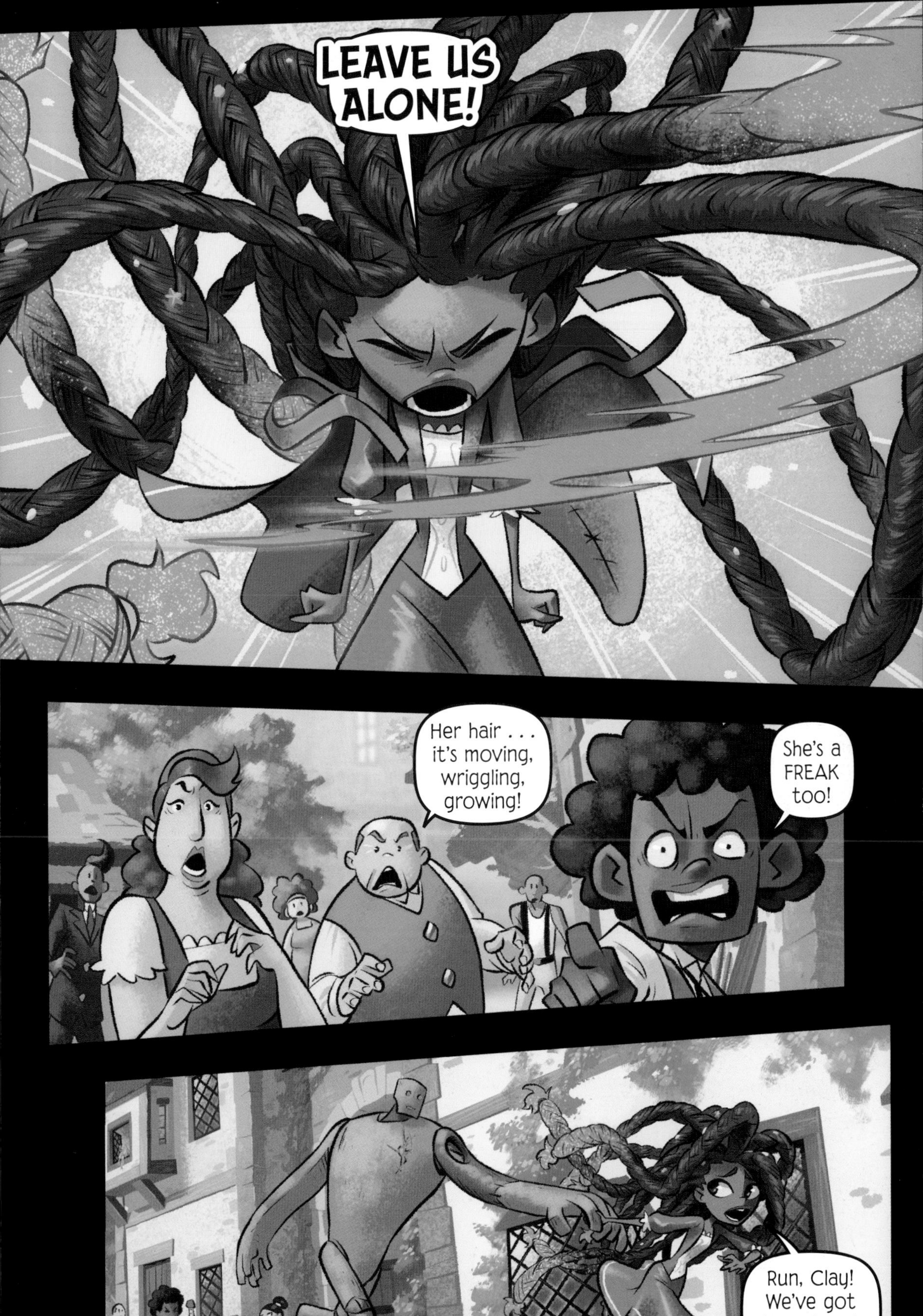
LEAVE US ALONE!
Her hair . . . it's moving, wriggling, growing!
She's a FREAK too!
Run, Clay! We've got to get out of here!

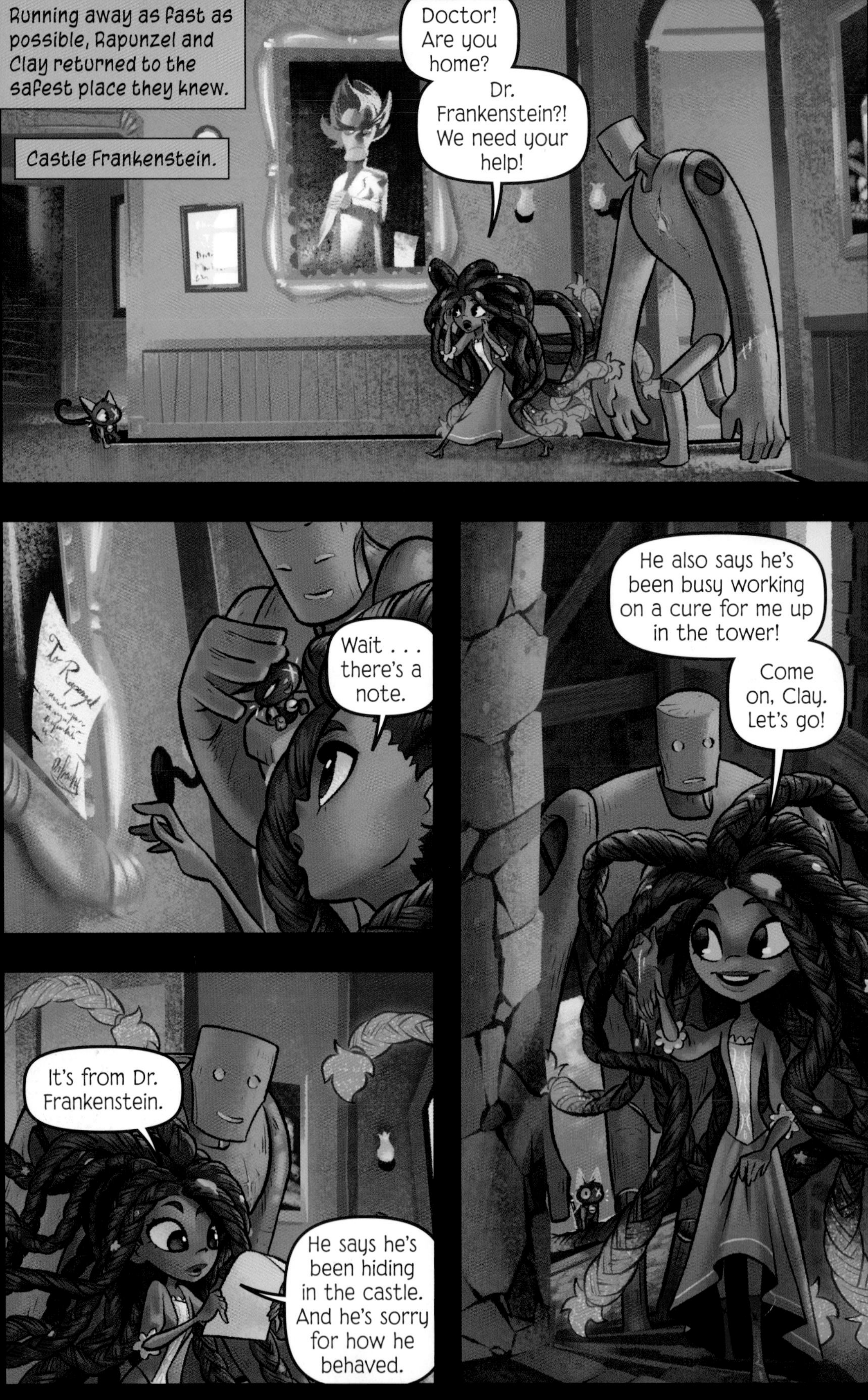
Running away as fast as possible, Rapunzel and Clay returned to the safest place they knew.
Castle Frankenstein.
Doctor! Are you home?
Dr. Frankenstein?! We need your help!
Wait . . . there's a note.
It's from Dr. Frankenstein.
He says he's been hiding in the castle. And he's sorry for how he behaved.
He also says he's been busy working on a cure for me up in the tower!
Come on, Clay. Let's go!

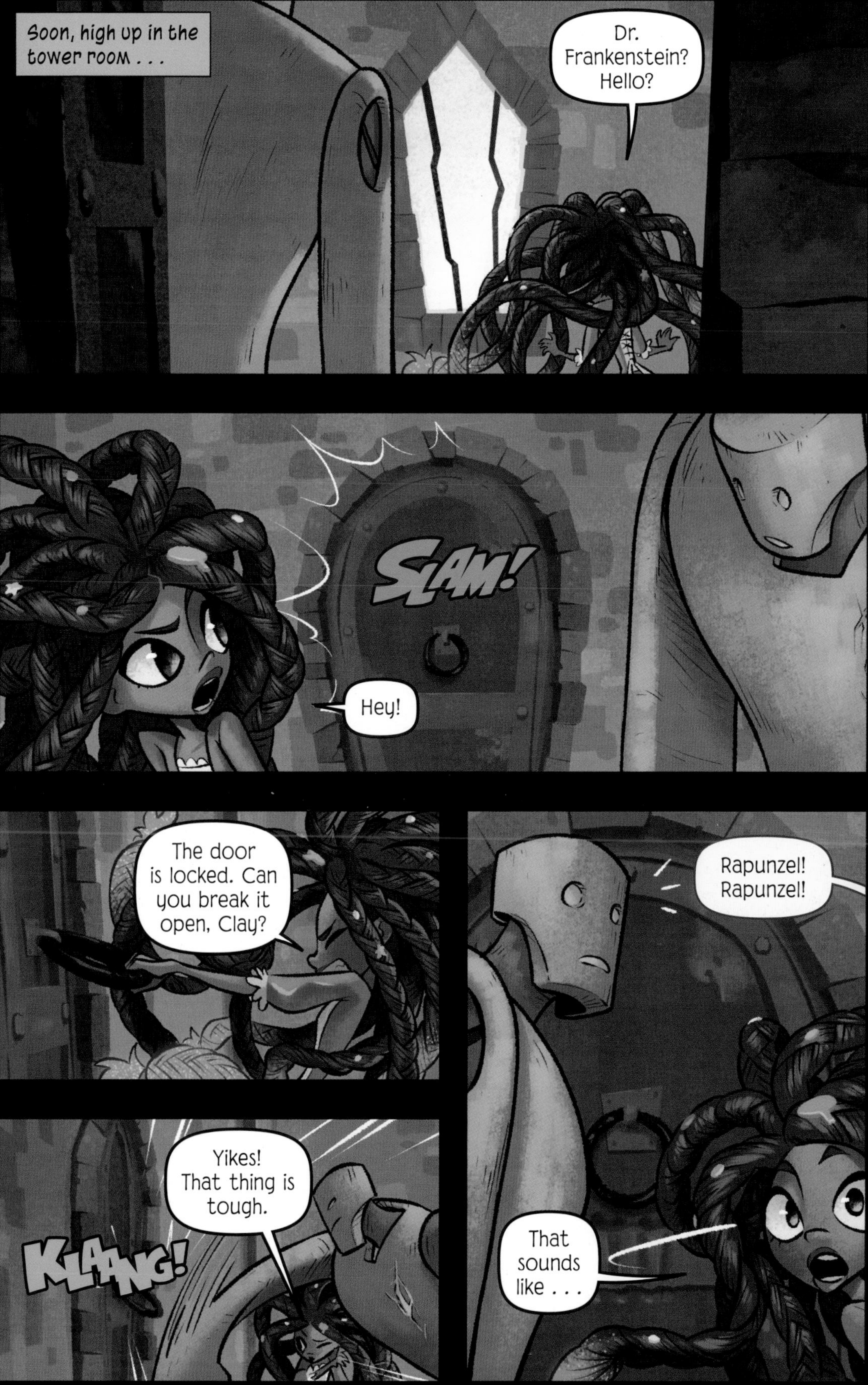
Soon, high up in the tower room . . .
Dr. Frankenstein? Hello?
SLAM!
Hey!
The door is locked. Can you break it open, Clay?
KLAAANG!
Yikes! That thing is tough.
Rapunzel! Rapunzel!
That sounds like . . .

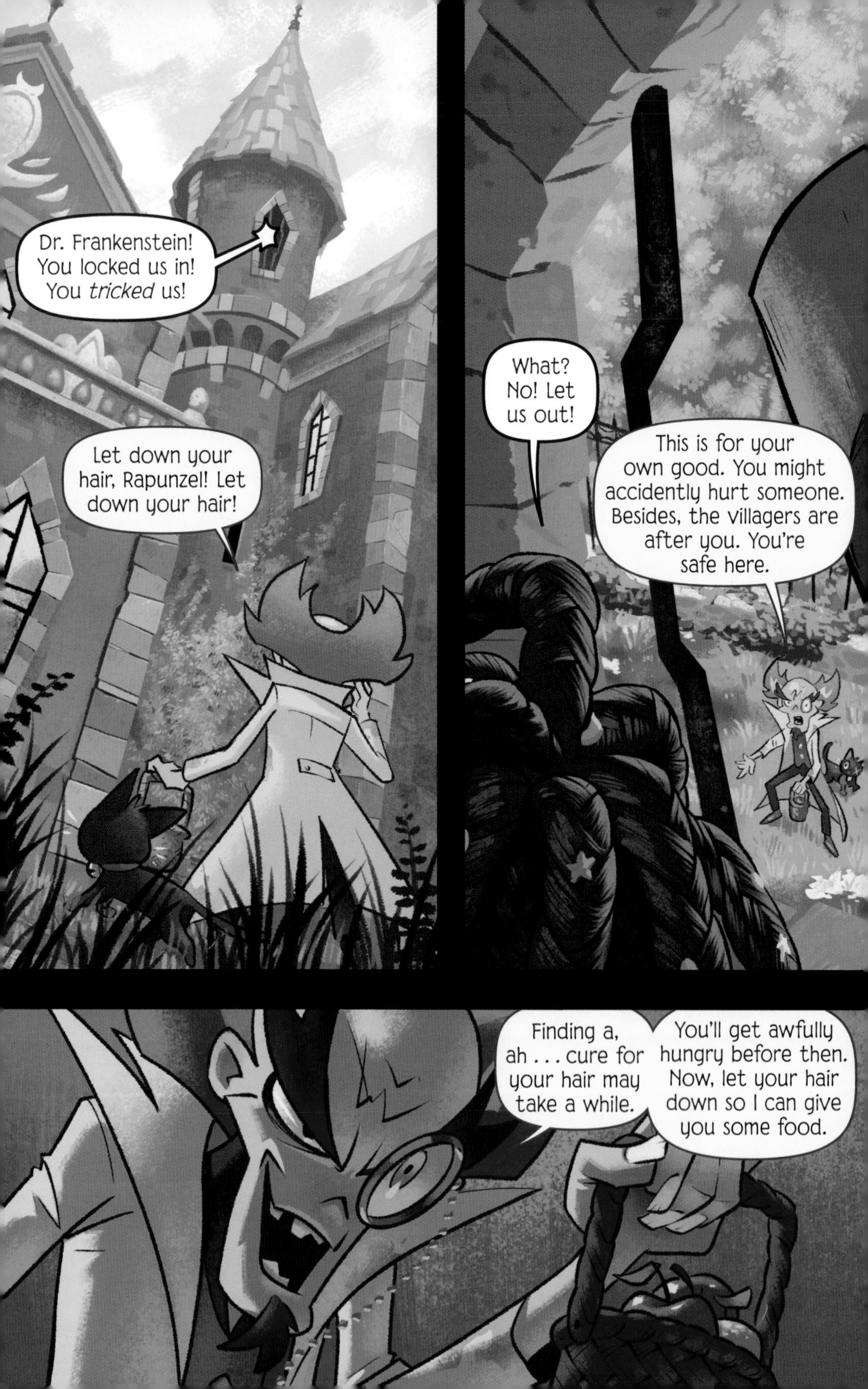
Dr. Frankenstein! You locked us in! You *tricked* us!
Let down your hair, Rapunzel! Let down your hair!
What? No! Let us out!
This is for your own good. You might accidently hurt someone. Besides, the villagers are after you. You're safe here.
Finding a, ah . . . cure for your hair may take a while.
You'll get awfully hungry before then. Now, let your hair down so I can give you some food.

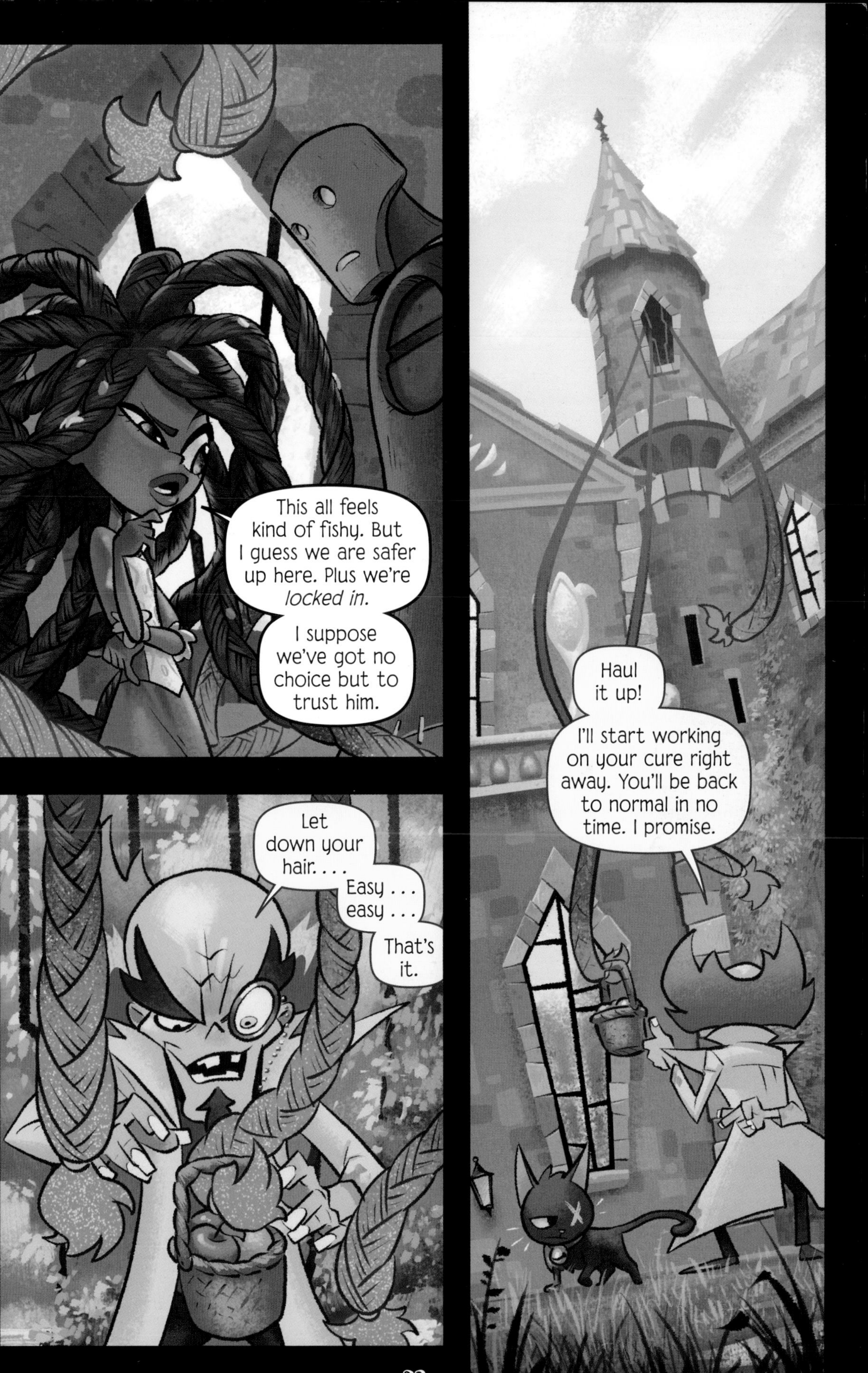
This all feels kind of fishy. But I guess we are safer up here. Plus we're *locked in.*
I suppose we've got no choice but to trust him.
Let down your hair. . . .
Easy . . . easy . . .
That's it.
Haul it up!
I'll start working on your cure right away. You'll be back to normal in no time. I promise.

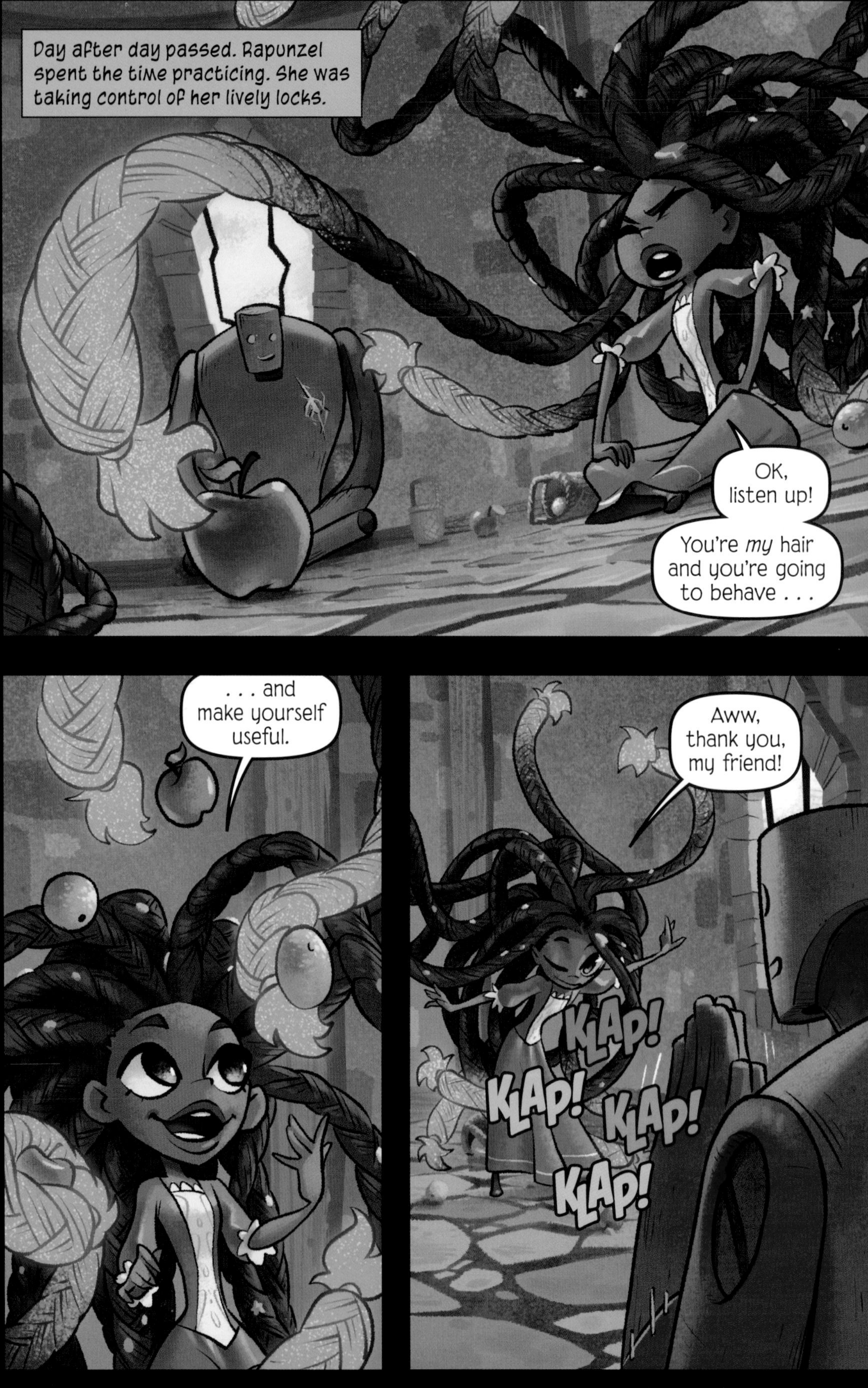

Day after day passed. Rapunzel spent the time practicing. She was taking control of her lively locks.
OK, listen up!
You're *my* hair and you're going to behave . . .
. . . and make yourself useful.
Aww, thank you, my friend!
KLAP!
KLAP!
KLAP!
KLAP!

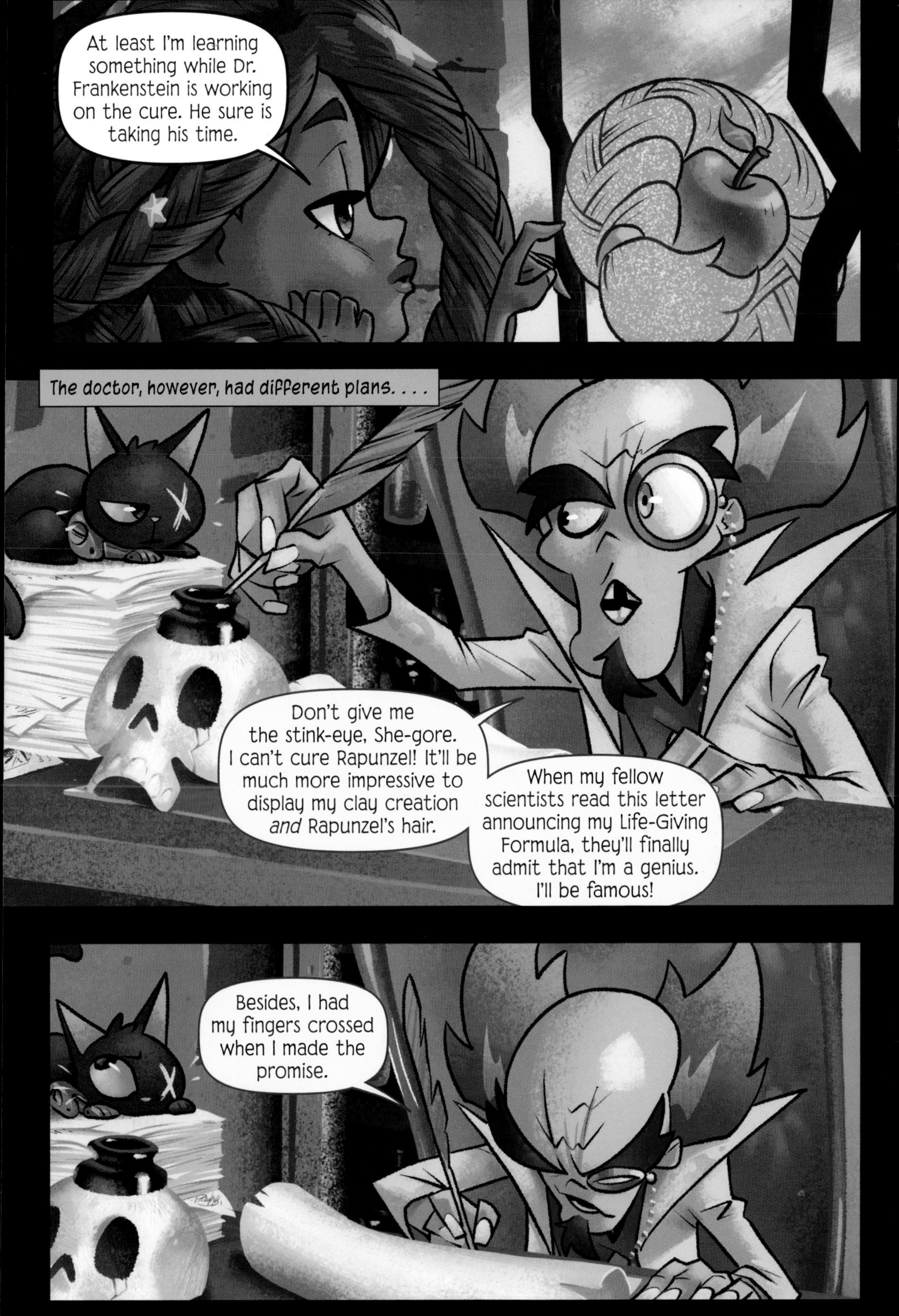
At least I'm learning something while Dr. Frankenstein is working on the cure. He sure is taking his time.
The doctor, however, had different plans. . . .
Don't give me the stink-eye, She-gore. I can't cure Rapunzel! It'll be much more impressive to display my clay creation *and* Rapunzel's hair.
When my fellow scientists read this letter announcing my Life-Giving Formula, they'll finally admit that I'm a genius. I'll be famous!
Besides, I had my fingers crossed when I made the promise.

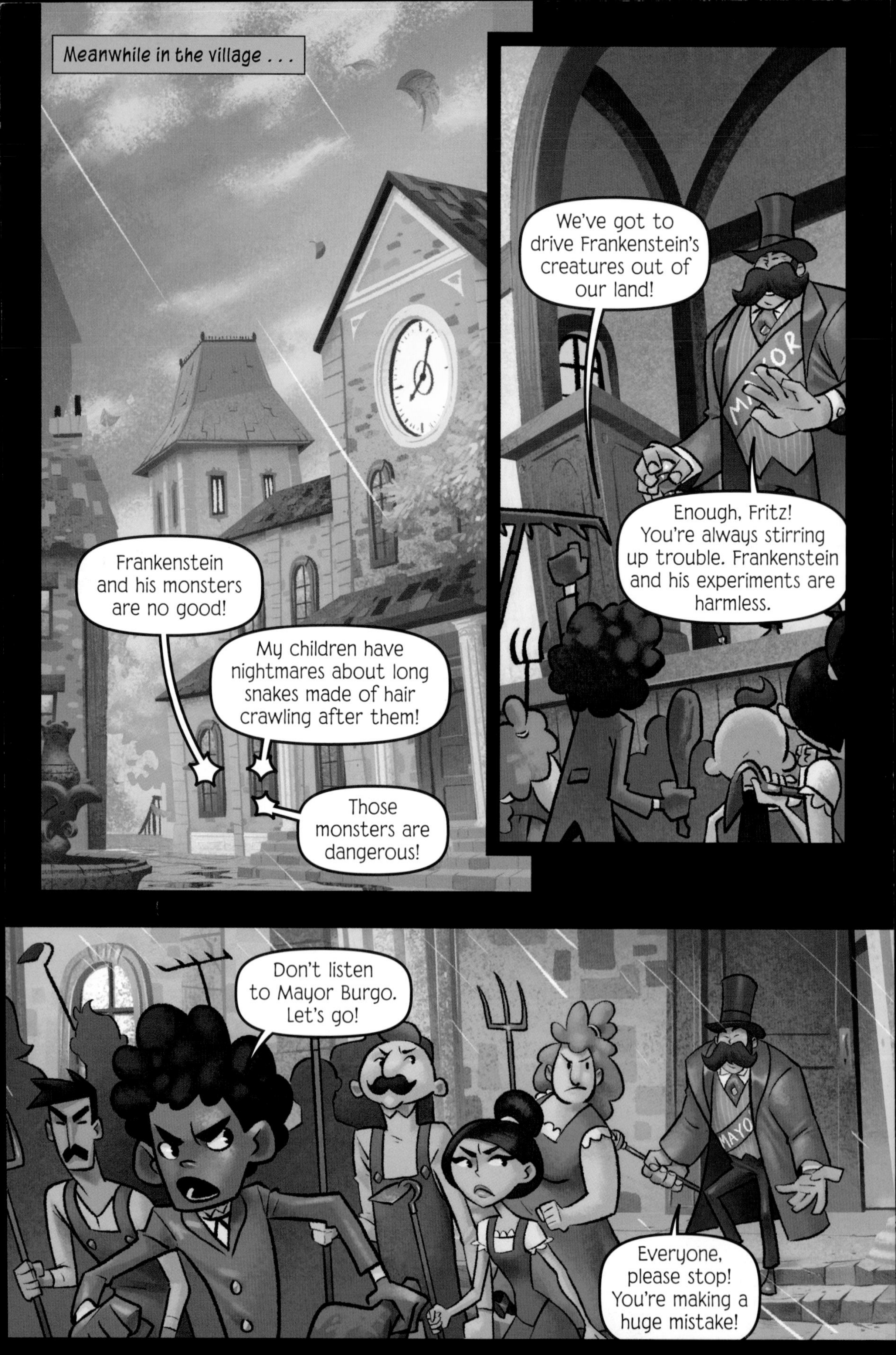
Meanwhile in the village . . .
Frankenstein and his monsters are no good!
My children have nightmares about long snakes made of hair crawling after them!
Those monsters are dangerous!
We've got to drive Frankenstein's creatures out of our land!
MAYOR
Enough, Fritz! You're always stirring up trouble. Frankenstein and his experiments are harmless.
Don't listen to Mayor Burgo. Let's go!
Everyone, please stop! You're making a huge mistake!

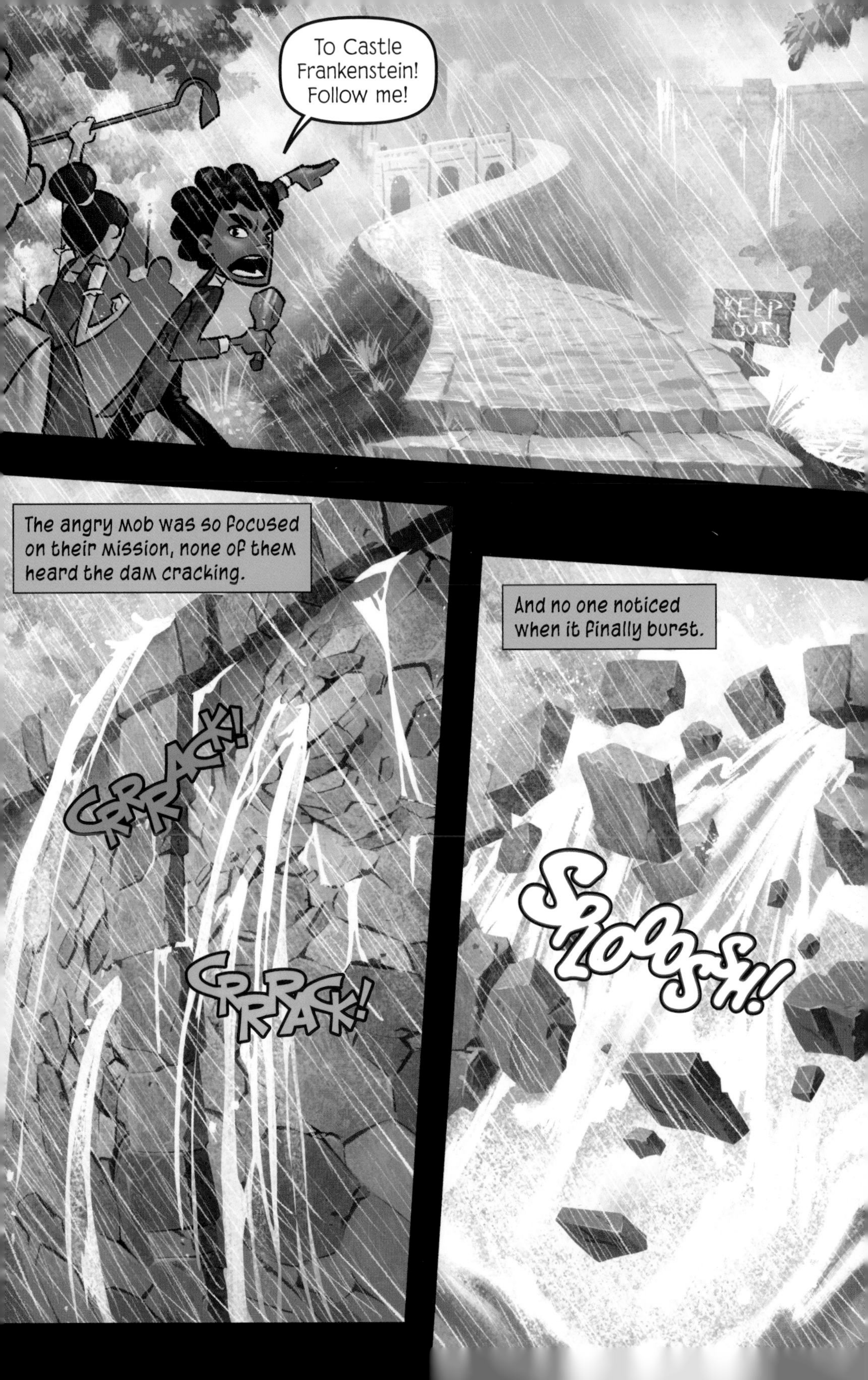
To Castle Frankenstein! Follow me!
KEEP OUT!
The angry mob was so focused on their mission, none of them heard the dam cracking.
CRRRACK!
CRRRACK!
And no one noticed when it finally burst.
SPLOOOSH!

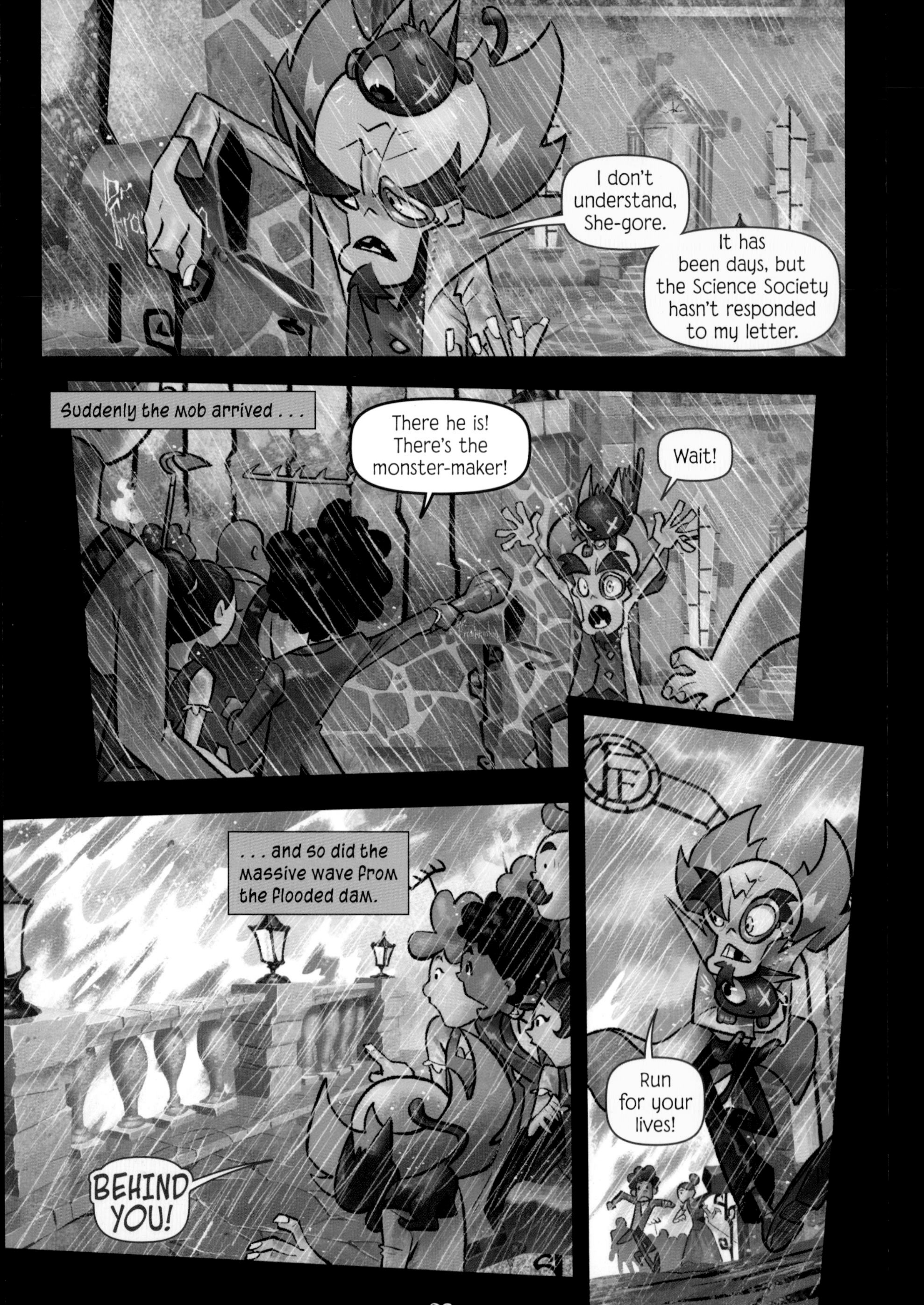
I don't understand, She-gore.
It has been days, but the Science Society hasn't responded to my letter.
Suddenly the mob arrived . . .
There he is! There's the monster-maker!
Wait!
. . . and so did the massive wave from the flooded dam.
BEHIND YOU!
Run for your lives!

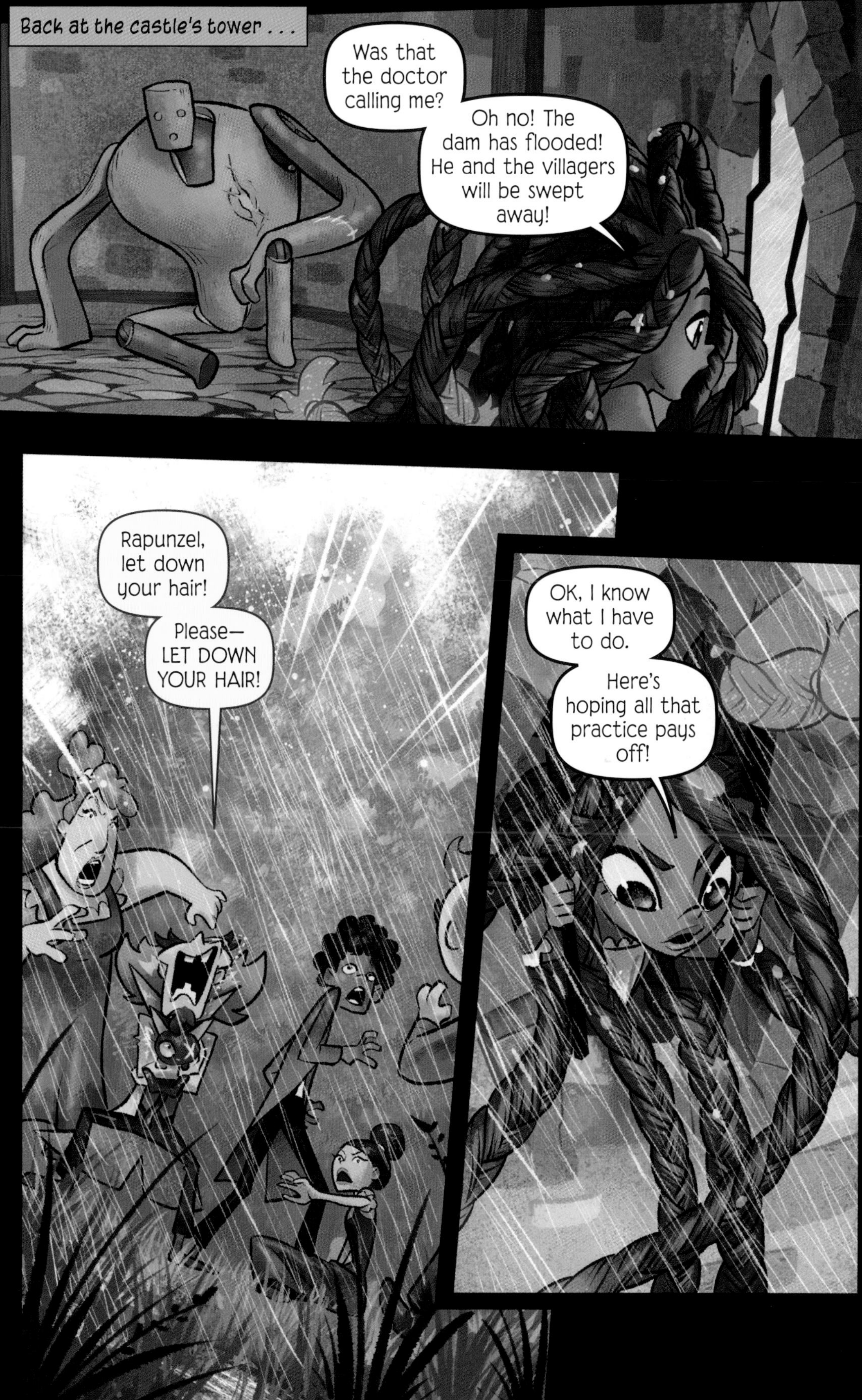
Back at the castle's tower . . .
Was that the doctor calling me?
Oh no! The dam has flooded! He and the villagers will be swept away!
Rapunzel, let down your hair!
Please— LET DOWN YOUR HAIR!
OK, I know what I have to do.
Here's hoping all that practice pays off!

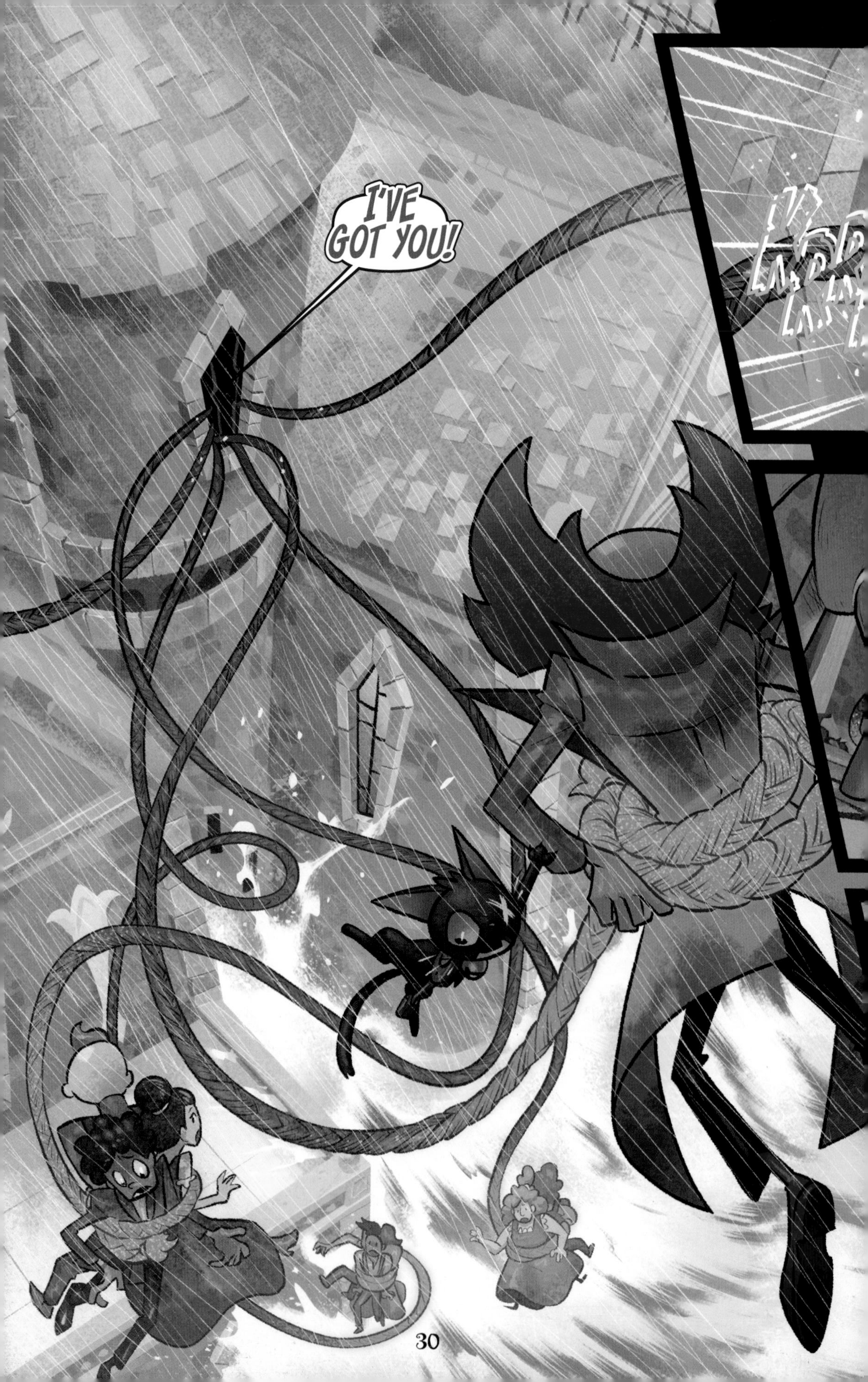
I'VE GOT YOU!

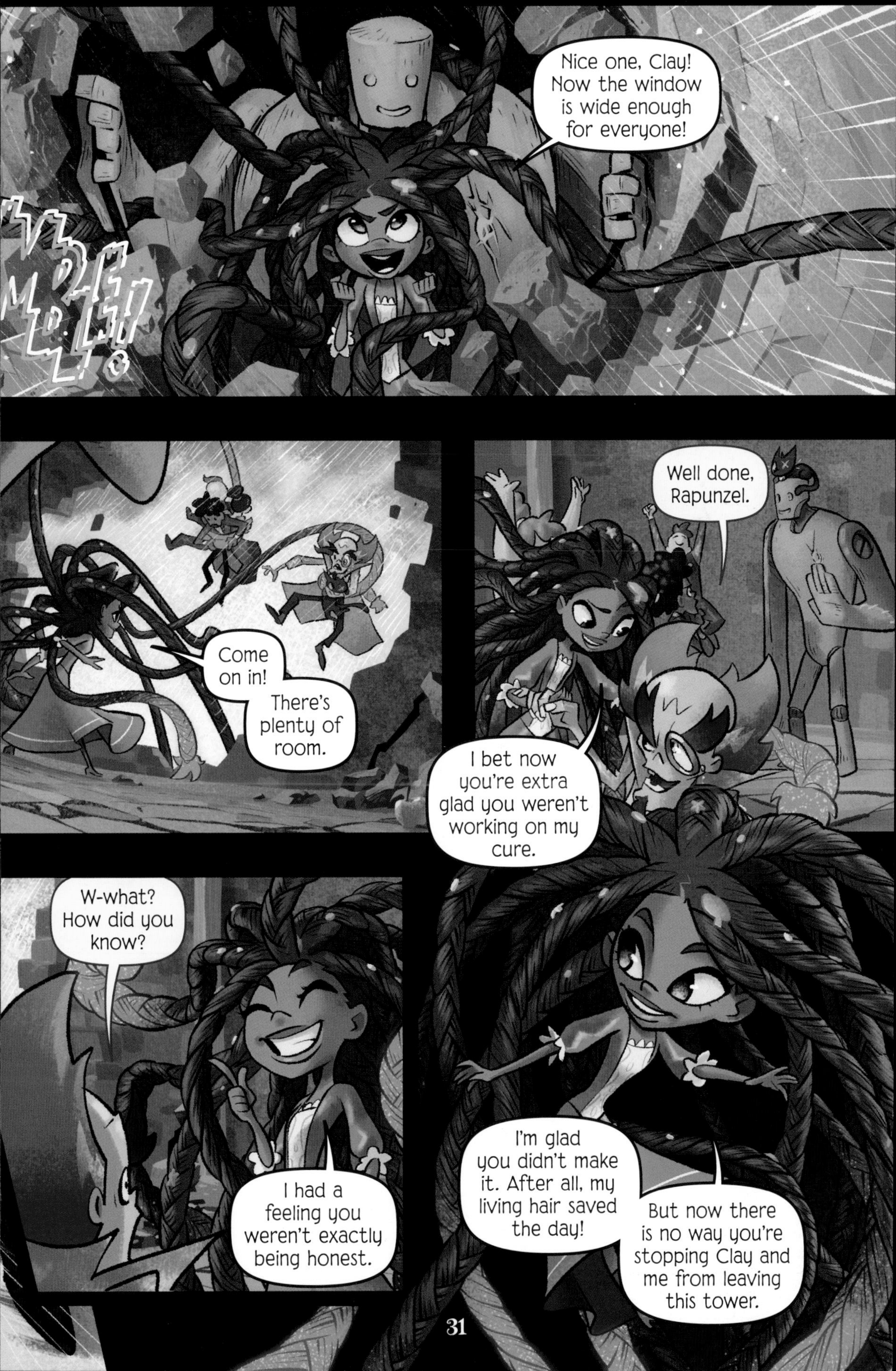
Nice one, Clay! Now the window is wide enough for everyone!
Come on in!
There's plenty of room.
Well done, Rapunzel.
I bet now you're extra glad you weren't working on my cure.
W-what? How did you know?
I had a feeling you weren't exactly being honest.
I'm glad you didn't make it. After all, my living hair saved the day!
But now there is no way you're stopping Clay and me from leaving this tower.

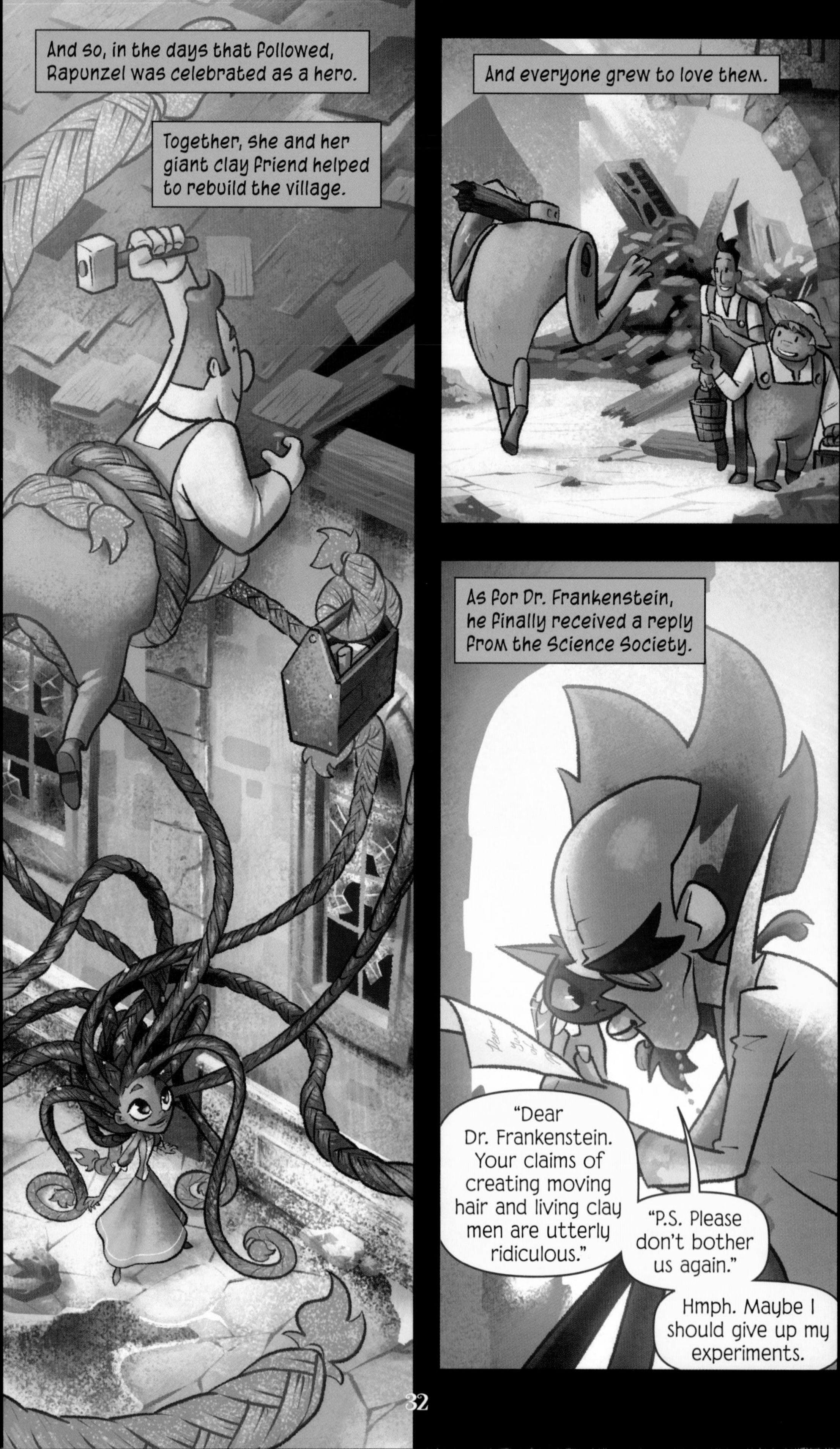

And so, in the days that followed, Rapunzel was celebrated as a hero.
Together, she and her giant clay friend helped to rebuild the village.
And everyone grew to love them.
As for Dr. Frankenstein, he finally received a reply from the Science Society.
"Dear Dr. Frankenstein. Your claims of creating moving hair and living clay men are utterly ridiculous."
"P.S. Please don't bother us again."
Hmph. Maybe I should give up my experiments.

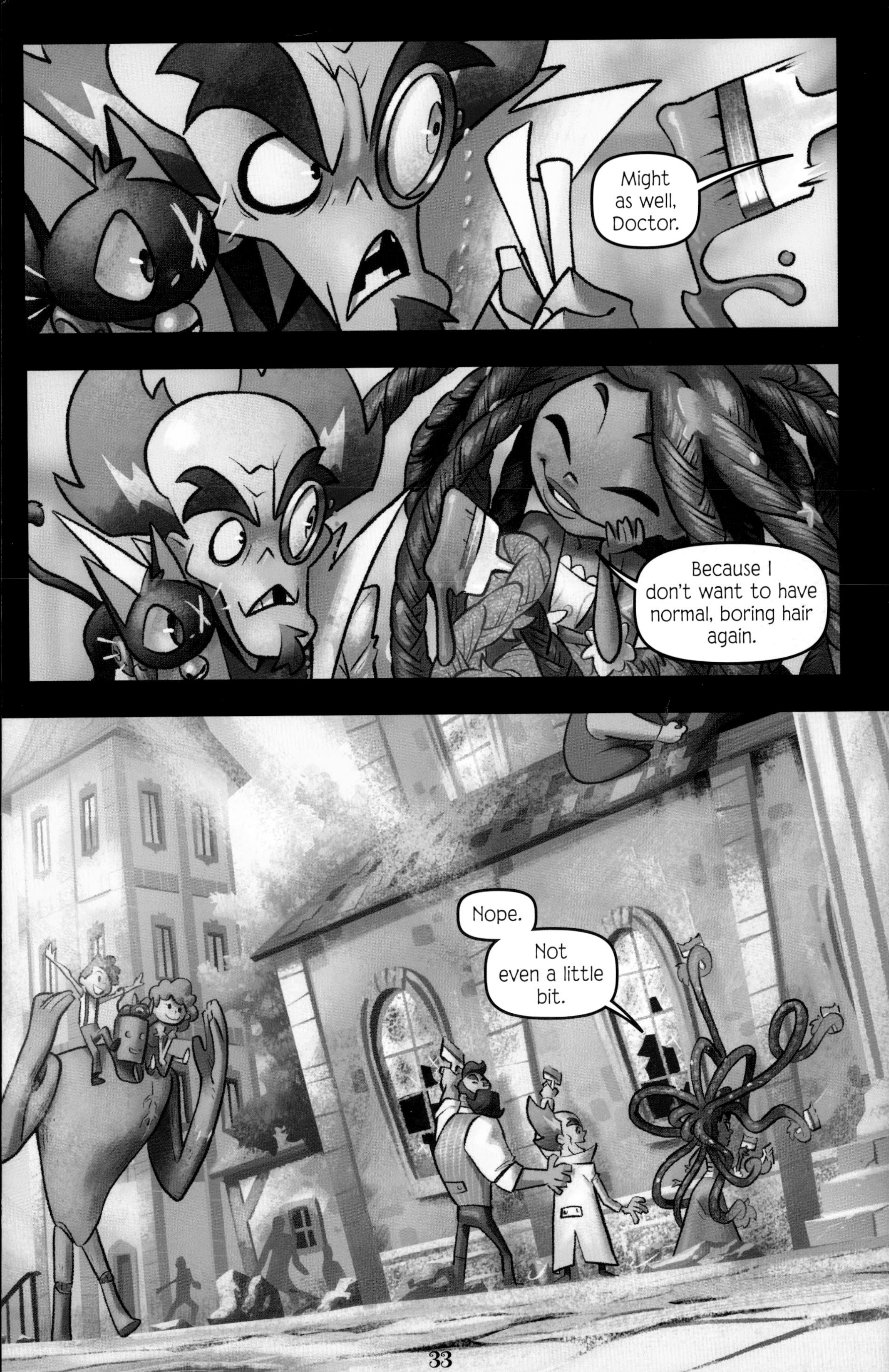
Might as well, Doctor.
Because I don't want to have normal, boring hair again.
Nope.
Not even a little bit.

ALL ABOUT THE ORIGINAL TALE!

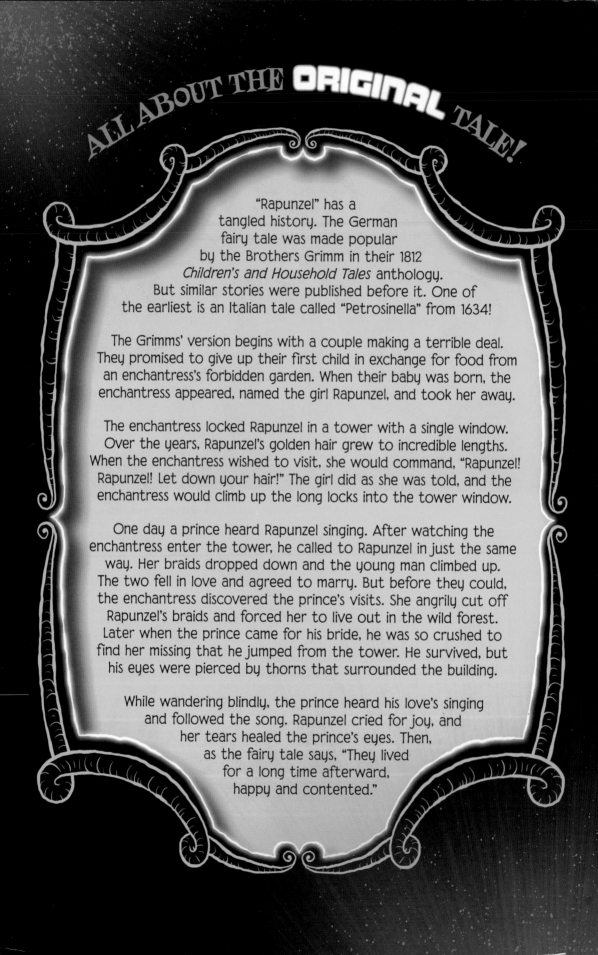

"Rapunzel" has a tangled history. The German fairy tale was made popular by the Brothers Grimm in their 1812 *Children's and Household Tales* anthology. But similar stories were published before it. One of the earliest is an Italian tale called "Petrosinella" from 1634!

The Grimms' version begins with a couple making a terrible deal. They promised to give up their first child in exchange for food from an enchantress's forbidden garden. When their baby was born, the enchantress appeared, named the girl Rapunzel, and took her away.

The enchantress locked Rapunzel in a tower with a single window. Over the years, Rapunzel's golden hair grew to incredible lengths. When the enchantress wished to visit, she would command, "Rapunzel! Rapunzel! Let down your hair!" The girl did as she was told, and the enchantress would climb up the long locks into the tower window.

One day a prince heard Rapunzel singing. After watching the enchantress enter the tower, he called to Rapunzel in just the same way. Her braids dropped down and the young man climbed up. The two fell in love and agreed to marry. But before they could, the enchantress discovered the prince's visits. She angrily cut off Rapunzel's braids and forced her to live out in the wild forest. Later when the prince came for his bride, he was so crushed to find her missing that he jumped from the tower. He survived, but his eyes were pierced by thorns that surrounded the building.

While wandering blindly, the prince heard his love's singing and followed the song. Rapunzel cried for joy, and her tears healed the prince's eyes. Then, as the fairy tale says, "They lived for a long time afterward, happy and contented."

A FAR OUT GUIDE TO THE TALE'S FRANKENSTEIN TWISTS!

Rapunzel's hair isn't just super long—it's also alive!

Instead of being rescued by a prince, Rapunzel saves the villagers, Dr. Frankenstein, and herself!

The cruel and selfish enchantress is replaced by Dr. Frankenstein, an equally selfish inventor.

In the original, Rapunzel's hair is cut off. In this version, Rapunzel accepts her moving hair and it becomes a positive part of who she is.

VISUAL QUESTIONS

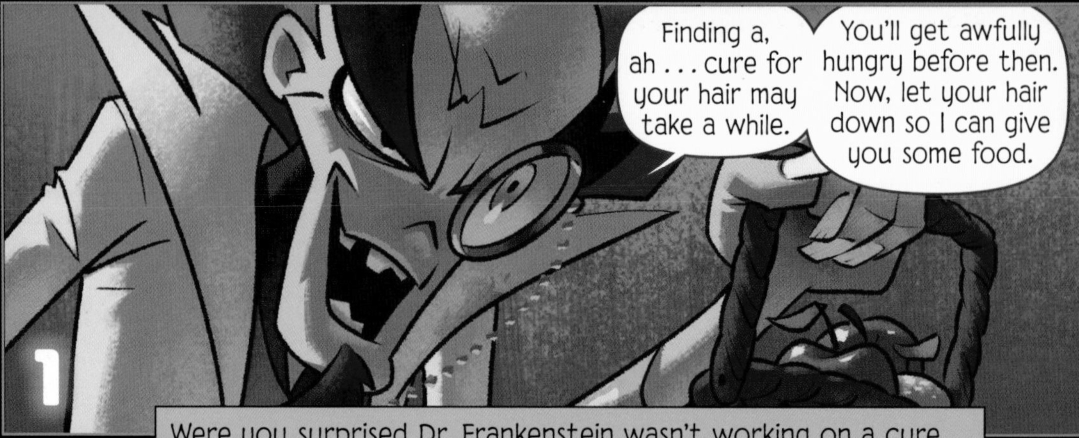
1
Finding a, ah . . . cure for your hair may take a while.
You'll get awfully hungry before then. Now, let your hair down so I can give you some food.

Were you surprised Dr. Frankenstein wasn't working on a cure for Rapunzel? Look at this panel from page 22. How do the art and text hint that the doctor isn't being honest? Talk about it!

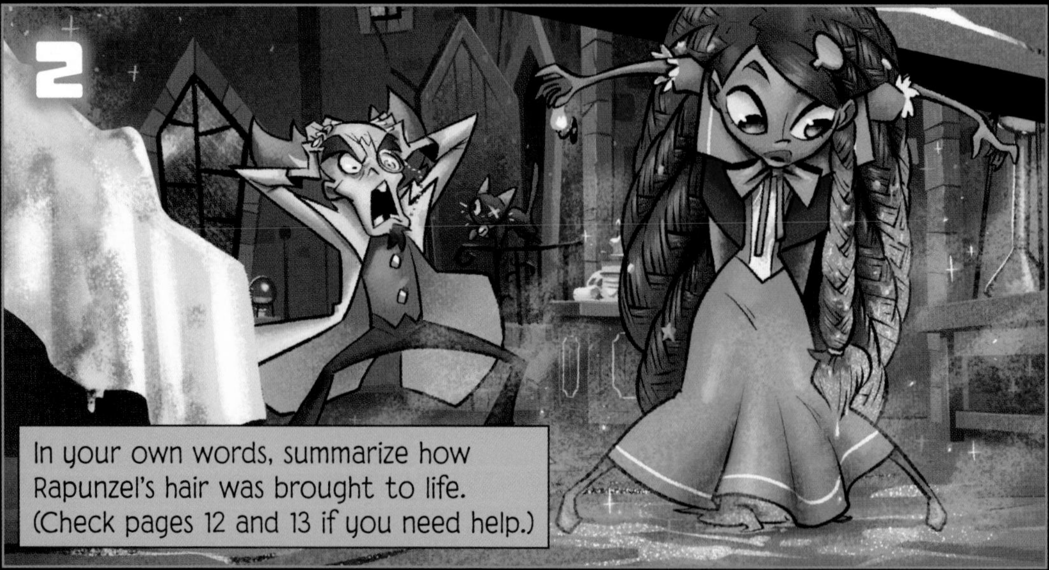
2

In your own words, summarize how Rapunzel's hair was brought to life. (Check pages 12 and 13 if you need help.)

How did Rapunzel first feel about her living hair? How do her feelings change throughout the story? Write two paragraphs about it, and be sure to use examples from the text and art.

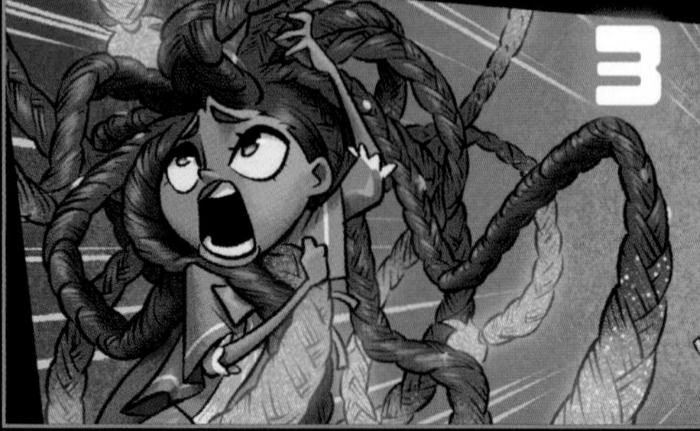
3

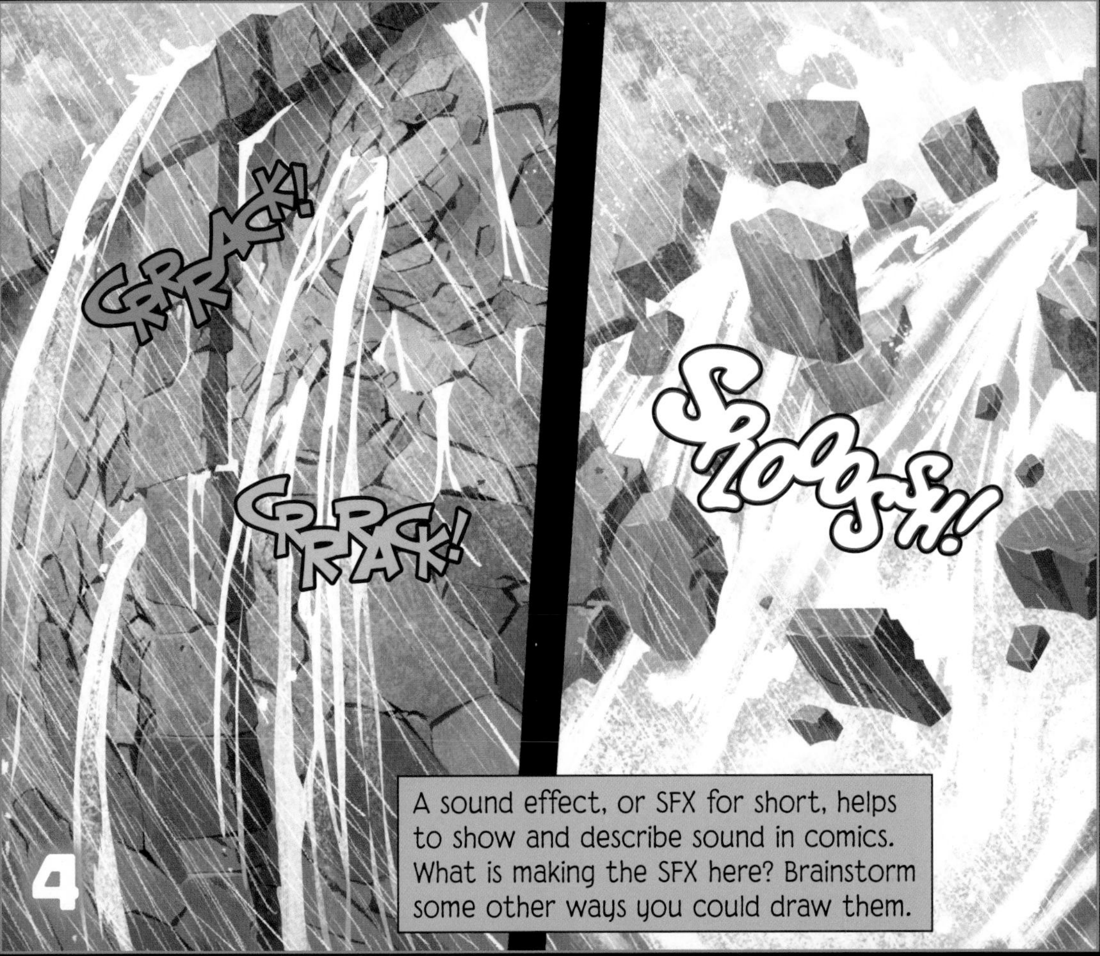
CRRRACK!
CRRRACK!
SPLOOSH!
4
A sound effect, or SFX for short, helps to show and describe sound in comics. What is making the SFX here? Brainstorm some other ways you could draw them.

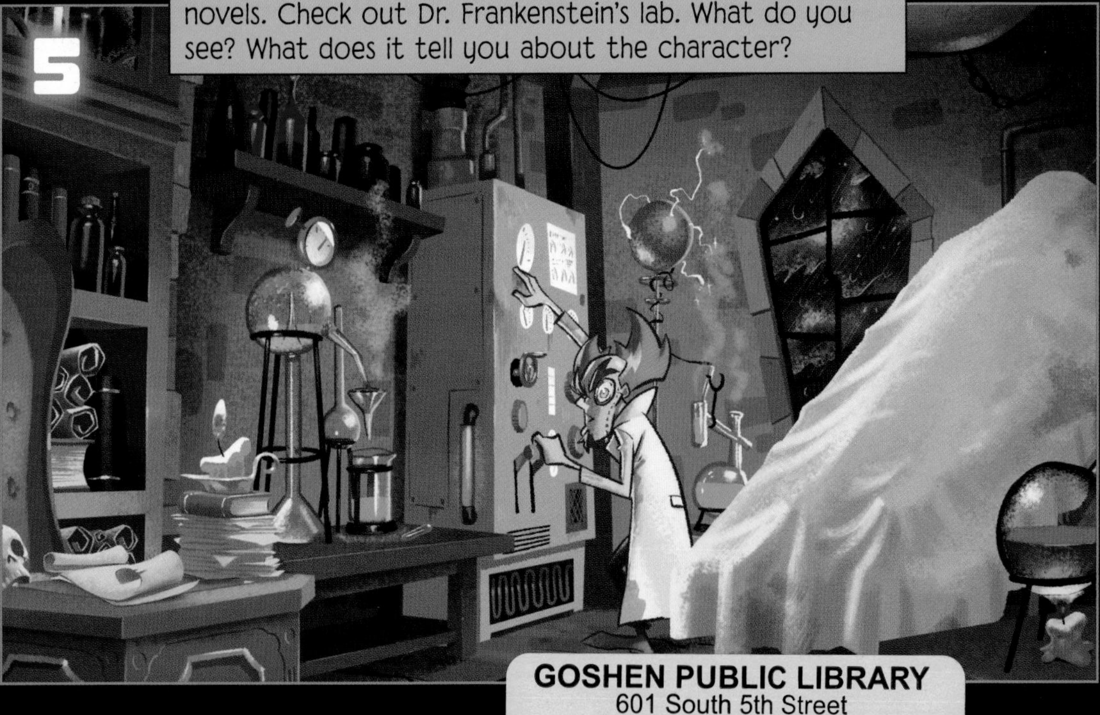
You can get a lot of information from the art in graphic novels. Check out Dr. Frankenstein's lab. What do you see? What does it tell you about the character?
5

AUTHOR

Martin Powell is the author of more than twenty children's books including *The Tall Tale of Paul Bunyan*, which won the national Moonbeam Gold Award for Best Children's Graphic Novel of 2010. Powell is the creator of *The Halloween Legion*, a nominee for the Stan Lee Excelsior Award, and also an educational writer for Gander Publishing, dedicated to improving literacy reading skills for students of all ages. In 2017, he received the coveted Golden Lion Award from The Burroughs Bibliophiles for his on-going contributions to the legacy of the adventure and sci-fi novelist Edgar Rice Burroughs.

ILLUSTRATOR

Omar Lozano lives in Monterrey, Mexico. He has always been crazy for illustration and is constantly on the lookout for awesome things to draw. In his free time, he watches lots of movies, reads fantasy and sci-fi books, and draws! Omar has worked for Marvel Comics, DC Comics, IDW, Dark Horse Comics, Capstone, and several other publishing companies.

GLOSSARY

collapse (kuh-LAPS)—to fall apart completely and suddenly

creation (kree-AY-shuhn)—something new that has been made, often through human skill and imagination

cure (KYOOR)—to make healthy; a cure is also something that stops a sickness or ends a problem

dam (DAM)—a wall built across a river to hold back water

display (dih-SPLAY)—to show off something in a way so that it is easily seen by others

experiment (ik-SPEER-uh-muhnt)—a scientific test to find out how something works

formula (FOR-myoo-luh)—a list of the ingredients used for making something (like a secret life-giving mixture!)

lock (LOK)—a bit of hair

mob (MOB)—a large group of people who are angry, violent, or difficult to control

ridiculous (ri-DIK-yuh-luhs)—extremely silly, unbelievable, and going against common sense

society (suh-SAHY-uh-tee)—an organized group of people who have come together because of a common interest or purpose

AWESOME

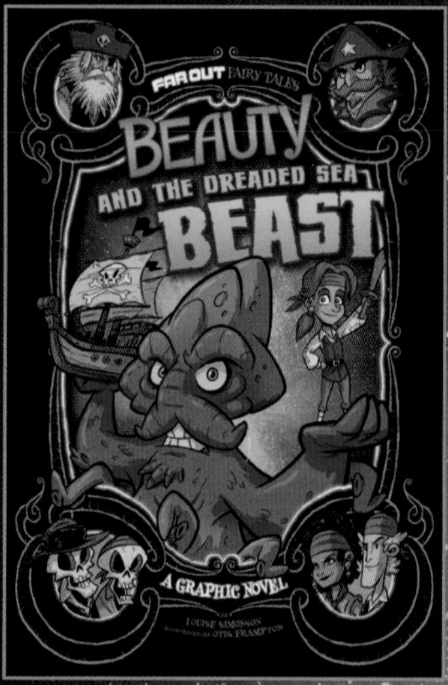
FAR OUT FAIRY TALES
BEAUTY AND THE DREADED SEA BEAST
A GRAPHIC NOVEL

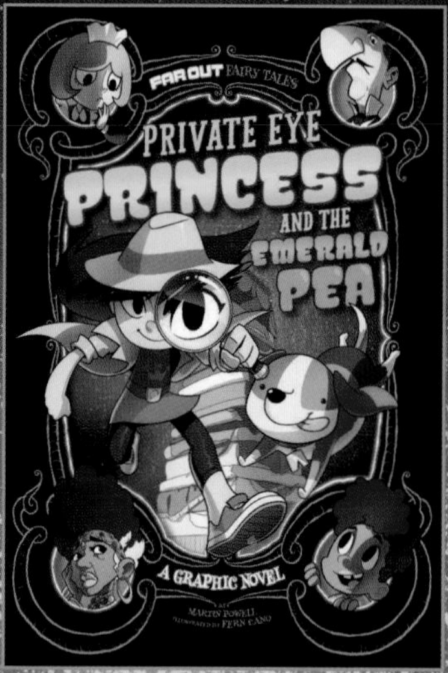
FAR OUT FAIRY TALES
PRIVATE EYE PRINCESS AND THE EMERALD PEA
A GRAPHIC NOVEL

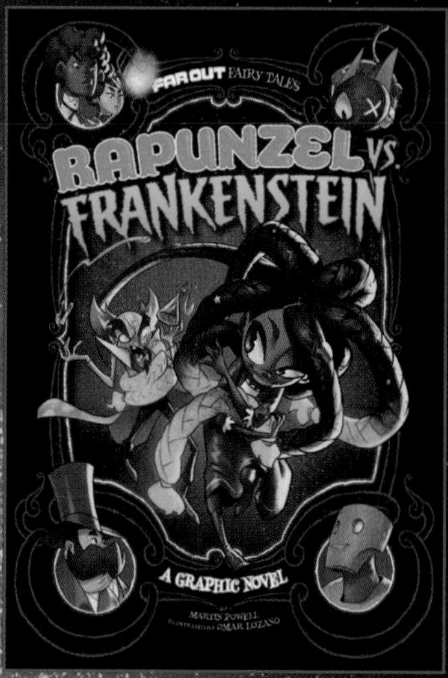
FAR OUT FAIRY TALES
RAPUNZEL VS. FRANKENSTEIN
A GRAPHIC NOVEL

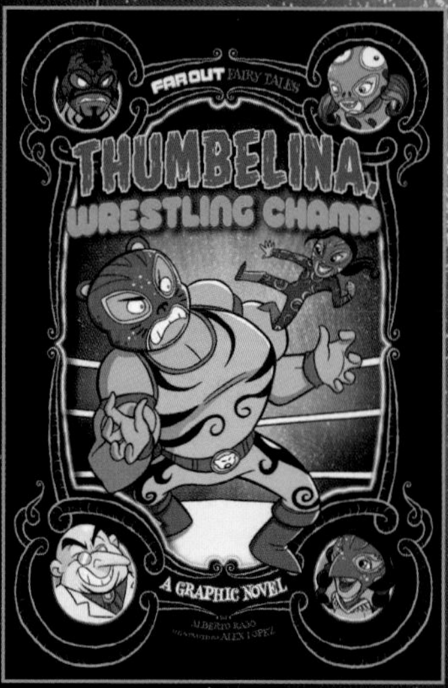
FAR OUT FAIRY TALES
THUMBELINA, WRESTLING CHAMP
A GRAPHIC NOVEL

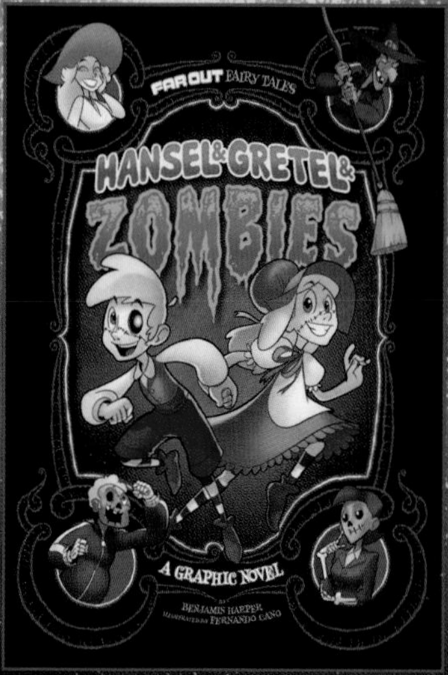
FAR OUT FAIRY TALES
HANSEL & GRETEL & ZOMBIES
A GRAPHIC NOVEL

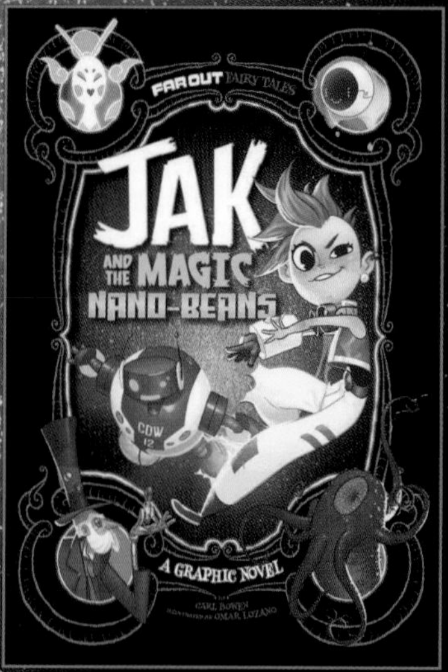
FAR OUT FAIRY TALES
JAK AND THE MAGIC NANO-BEANS
A GRAPHIC NOVEL

FAR OUT FAIRY TALES

ONLY FROM CAPSTONE!